HIDDEN HERITAGE

By

LIONEL ROSS

Also by the author: -

Fine Feathers
978-0-9552404-2-3

The Baghdad Declaration
978-0-9552404-1-6

Men of Conviction
978-0-9560369-3-3

The Dalethorpe Chronicles
978-0-9560369-7-1

Hidden Heritage

978-0-9552404-1-6

Published by:
i2i Publishing
Manchester M25 0NL UK
www.i2ipublishing.co.uk

First edition 2006

Second (revised) edition 2010

Third Impression 2011

CHAPTER ONE

THE ALVARO FAMILY

CORDOVA 1492

The filthy rivers of mud that passed for roads during the winter were now drying out. The warm sun of the short Spanish springtime would soon give way to the baking heat of the long hot summer. Mercifully, much of the mud had already hardened as the sun had an unusual ally in its annual task of baking the roads. The drying mud was being compacted as it dried by the footsteps of a vast multitude of men and beasts trudging tortuously westwards. From time to time the uneven surface caused the few carriages and carts on the road to lurch and rattle but the surefootedness of the horses and donkeys that pulled the vehicles enabled them to stabilise and maintain a reasonable progress towards the distant destinations.

Alas, the pedestrians, the majority of this traffic, fared far worse than did those who were fortunate enough to be able to ride. There were still large pools of dirty, stinking black water for them to cross between the areas of baked mud. To avoid a drenching in the revolting liquid the pedestrians quickly learned to keep a safe distance between themselves and the carriage wheels. Most of these people had started their journey in brightly coloured clothing. This had now been transformed into a uniform, dismal grey. The trudging majority pushed or pulled handcarts on which were piled as many of their treasured possessions as they could safely stack. These sad bundles represented the pitiful remnant of generations of endeavour in the country of their birth.

Don Jose Alvaro or Yosef ben Shimon, as he preferred to be called, together with his wife, Rebecca and their three children, has started their journey in their hometown of Cordoba. Don Jose was reputed to be a wealthy man. His Spanish servants had helped the family to load their clothing and personal effects into whatever available space they could find. Not only the interior of the large, luxurious carriage but also the roof, was piled high with their belongings. There was just enough room for the five members of the family with the men seated on top and the ladies within.

The servants had wept and Rebecca and the children had wept at this sudden cruel parting. Manuel and Maria were simple people whose families had served the Alvaro clan for generations. They had always been treated generously and felt more like Alvaro family members than like servants. So strong was the bond that when the edict was first heard in Cordoba, Manuel and Maria had wanted to accompany their employers into exile.

"No, no!" Jose has said, "Your place is here in Cordoba. Our ancestors may have been here for a thousand years but we Jews always knew that our truly permanent home could only be in the land of Israel."

"When we are told to move on," he continued sadly, "we must follow the will of God."

"Please let us come," Manuel begged, "our place is with you."

Jose realised he must be cruel to be kind and with a stern expression he countered,

"Don't you think I have enough people to worry about without you two?"

"Besides," he continued, "there will hardly be enough room for the family without extra baggage."

Manuel was hurt but when he finally embraced his master on the day of departure he understood how deeply grieved Jose felt by the enforced separation.

There had been Alvaros in the Iberian Peninsula for nearly fifteen hundred years. They were there when the Visigoths arrived and one of Jose's forebears had welcomed the Moors to Spain all of seven hundred years earlier.

The story of how this remarkable family came to be in Hispania, as the Romans called it, started with the destruction of Jerusalem by those same Romans. Yosef ben Azaria was a merchant in the Holy City, Jerusalem. Immediately before the final siege, he had transferred himself, his family and his not inconsiderable wealth to the coast of Judea, at a point near to the ancient port of Jaffa. From there he traded with the other main commercial centres in the Roman Empire. To assist this process he had despatched five of his six sons to open branches of the business, in those distant ports. His second and most able son, Aharon ben Yosef had been sent to a town in the north west of Hispania named after Cesar Augustus and eventually corrupted by the local population to be called Saragossa.

Aharon had prospered there and he and his wife Chana had produced nine children. Only the two daughters and the oldest son Chaim had remained in Saragossa. The other sons had all settled in towns further south in the large peninsula.

Other Jews or Judeans as they were then called had also been drawn to the opportunities that existed at this opposite end of the Mediterranean Sea. After the complete destruction of their beloved Jerusalem they knew that their future could only be built away from the ravages of war. The Romans were delighted to encourage this process. They had quickly discovered that outside their own land the Jews were a great asset to the Empire. In Judea they were permanently in rebellion but abroad they were intelligent, hard working and peaceable. They were in fact the only people to have their religion recognised by Rome alongside the heathen practices of the dominant power itself. It was not difficult therefore for the sons of Aharon to find wives from among the thousands of Jews already settled in Hispania. Their descendants prospered and spread throughout this new and fertile land.

The other inhabitants had, just like the Jews in Judea, fought long and hard against the Roman invaders but despite achieving amazing victories Hispania had eventually been pacified under the rule of Pax Romana. It was therefore, in this atmosphere that the Jews and early Iberians had been able to work together for the common good.

All this changed with the arrival of Christianity as the official religion of Rome. Suddenly, the Jews, the people, from whom their saviour had arisen, were seen to constitute a threat to the new faith. The fortunes of the Alvaro family and its co-religionists went into deep decline. The Visigoths who drove out the last of the Romans also treated the Jews badly. Somehow the Alvaro family survived and prayed for better times

In the year 711 their prayers were answered. A new era dawned for Spain and all its inhabitants with the arrival of the Moors from North Africa. They were a fierce people fired with the zeal of a new religion, Islam. At first they were seen as cruel conquerors but soon the Spaniards; Christians, Jews and heathens had to recognise the civilising force of these new arrivals. They quickly built new cities and towns. They traded throughout the known world. And most importantly they loved, respected and encouraged all forms of learning. They decreed that Christians and Jews, as peoples of the book, were to be allowed religious freedom as long as they did not attempt to convert Muslims to their faiths. They needed large numbers of lawyers, doctors, merchants and skilled artisans to build this new civilisation and the Jews were delighted to oblige. At last here was a people they could work alongside, people who seemed to share many of their values. Spain prospered and so did the Alvaro family.

The first record of members of the Alvaro family living in Cordoba dates back to the year 756 when that town was proclaimed capital of Muslim Spain or Al Andalus as the new conquerors called it. Apart from occasional setbacks the following centuries found the family enjoying increasing prosperity and honour. Indeed a distant ancestor of Don Jose had been minister of finance to Abd-el-Rahman the third and in the eleventh century another ancestor had been vizier to the King of Granada.

It must be said that other Jews including relatives of the Alvaro family, despite the Christian prejudice against them, also achieved great pre-eminence under the Christian Kings of the North Iberian Kingdoms.

Life was not always sweet under the Muslims. Jews and Christians alike had spent a number of very unhappy years after the invasion of a fanatical Muslim sect called the Almohads. However, this was but a ripple in the long history of Islamic rule and with the return of the Moorish Kings, life returned to its former state of relative tranquillity.

Eventually, the first signs of a change for the worse came with the arrival of the Crusaders from the North. The Alvaro family and their co-religionists found their position deteriorating rapidly as the Spanish Christians set out to drive the Infidel Moor from the land. Cordoba fell to the Christian armies in 1235. The head of the Alvaro family in the city at that time was a distinguished physician still known by his Arabic name of Yusuf Al Hakim. His care for the sick, rich and poor, Christian, Muslim and Jew had earned him the love and respect of the entire population.

The son of Yusuf was also a doctor and it was he who first took the surname of Alvaro. Succeeding generations settled down to work and serve the town under its new masters although now there was an increasing undercurrent of anti-Jewish feeling. The rulers of Christian Spain used the Jews as a scapegoat for the now vanished Muslims. It was easy to persuade the primitive peasant population that the same people, who, according to their priests, had killed their saviour, were in league against them with their other enemies the now vanquished Moors.

However, life was not all bad. Those Jews whose reputations were above character assassination still managed to prosper and to aid the majority of their brethren in the fight for survival. Those enjoying the patronage of the local rulers were able to intercede against the worst excesses of anti-Jewish legislation. Indeed, many members of the indigenous Christian population valued close friendships with Jewish families. This was hardly surprising as in the anti-Jewish riots of 1392 many Jews had felt it prudent to convert to the faith of Jesus and most of their descendants knew, or at least suspected, their own origins.

For the next hundred years this process continued and forced conversions were frequent in all parts of Spain. Most of these 'conversos' were less than sincere in their new religion and this in turn in 1478, gave rise to the 'Holy Inquisition' with all its torture and cruelty perpetrated in the name of the gentle Jewish carpenter from Nazareth.

The fanatical priests, who ran the Inquisition, murdered many of Don José's cousins. However those Jews who managed to remain true to their ancient faith were outside the authority of that evil empire.

The Alvaro family was rich and influential. They lived comfortably and in the late fifteenth century Don José's business connections were internationally respected. He was, however, a realist and he could sense the gathering storm with every fibre of his being.

"Rebecca," he constantly reminded his wife, "we are living very comfortably now but I have no illusions about the future."

"Oh, Jose," his wife would reply when faced with the ever more frequent warnings of her husband, "you are becoming obsessed by all the bad news from Madrid and Barcelona. This is still Cordoba in Andalusia and here, I am sure, we will continue to live as we did in the past, in comfort and security."

"My love," Jose gently reprimanded her, "I am sorry to say you are deluding yourself. With Ferdinand and Isabella on the throne of a united Spain, our days in this country are numbered."

Sadly, Jose was right. Once King Ferdinand had married Queen Isabella they had set themselves the task of uniting the entire land of Spain under their leadership. For this unity to succeed there could be only one religion in Spain, Roman Catholicism. Little by little all the remaining pockets of Muslim territory were overrun and on the second of January 1492 the last Moorish King surrendered the keys of the fine old city of Granada to their most Catholic Majesties. Thus the fate of not only the Muslims but also the Jews was sealed.

Now there was no argument from Rebecca. Secretly, Jose planned the final departure of the Alvaro family from Spain. Non-perishable foodstuffs were stored for the journey to the coast. They packed all other portable possessions in an endeavour to ensure a relatively comfortable life in their new home. The location of the new home was uncertain at this stage, as a number of options appeared to be open to them. For some years Jose had been converting valuables into Gold and other precious metals and jewels. He had also shipped large quantities of goods to his cousins in Italy, North Africa and the Turkish Empire. These goods were to be sold and the proceeds held in gold until Jose was able to call for them from the city in which they would finally settle. But in which country they would eventually arrive depended on factors beyond José's control at that time. His preference was for Italy but this depended on the availability of a ship to take them there. Jose little thought that he was embarking on a journey that would last for his descendants for five hundred years and would then achieve the most remarkable conclusion, beyond the wildest dreams of Jews at that time, resident anywhere in the known world.

Chapter Two

The Allbarrow Family

Ireland 1990

He was eighteen years old and his entire life had been spent within twenty-five or thirty miles of where he had been born and raised.

Joseph was the oldest of the six children of Aron and Mary Allbarrow. They were simple shepherds and they lived in a cramped, ramshackle stone house that a cursory glance could confirm, was hundreds of years old.

They had tended their sheep on the rough rock-strewn hills of McGillicuddys Reeks for generations and their home on the lowest part of the southern slope of Carrantuohill was vulnerable to the worst that the Atlantic Ocean could throw at the dwelling. Happily, both the house and its occupants were determined to withstand the twin onslaughts of the weather and of the twentieth century and certainly Aron, the head of the family, was confident that he could pass on the perceived benefits of his simple way of life to future generations.

Every Sunday, come rain or shine, the entire family would walk the five miles to the old Church in the village of Ballymagee. Only serious illness was accepted as a reason for non-attendance and minor coughs and colds certainly did not qualify. After Mass and Confession the Allbarrow family marched bravely back to their bleak hillside home to indulge in Bible readings and other suitable Sunday pursuits.

Television was completely banned from the house. It was considered by Aron to be an instrument of the devil and one of, if not the greatest, source of evil in the modern world.

The only concession to twentieth century pursuits was the radio. Aron's late father, also called Joseph, had consented to a tabletop model being introduced into the house but its use was limited strictly to Church programmes, News and 'suitable' music. Jazz, Pop, Rock'n Roll and their ilk were deemed to be sounds heralding an approaching Armageddon.

Aron had strenuously maintained his policy on Television even when his son Joseph and the other children had told him that their school friends used Television for educational purposes.

"And Dad," Joseph had pleaded, "It does not have to be expensive. You can pay off or rent a set from the shop in the village."

"Enough," Aron had bellowed. "We are a God fearing family. Once we have Television it would be the end of this family and of our way of life."

The house had only been connected to the electricity supply in the nineteen fifties. Joseph senior had agonised for many weeks before finally agreeing to accept it. He was sure that it ran contrary to the laws of God but the promise of relief from the bitter cold of that winter finally convinced him.

Cooking continued until the present day in an oven heated by the filthy, smouldering peat fire and this primitive form of power also heated the water for the weekly family bathing session that occupied the whole of every Saturday evening. First, the youngest and smallest were bathed in the large tin tub in front of the fire, two of the same sex at a time. Only Joseph and his oldest sister were allowed to bathe separately and in privacy. Finally Aron and Mary took their individual baths while each spouse waited alternately outside the living room door. Outside of the heavy sheets and blankets of the matrimonial bed there was no intimacy allowed or even sought between them.

The only contribution to the twentieth century was the fact that the older children were allowed the use of two ancient bicycles Aron had purchased some fifteen years earlier.

To the neighbouring village people the Allbarrows were known as fanatical Catholics. Apart from attending Church every Sunday and Saints Day they kept to the minutiae of the religion with zeal uncommon even in Southern Ireland. Three or four times a year Father Patrick Meadows from the village church would cycle over the overgrown hilly paths to visit the family. He was a distant kinsman but then at least a quarter of the villagers of Ballymagee were distantly related. He often wished and prayed that his other parishioners would be even half as devout as the Allbarrows in the stone cottage. Secretly though, he did not enjoy the visits to the family as even he found the sanctimonious piety of Aron hard to stomach.

The stone house consisted of just four rooms and was of course single storey. The largest room was used as kitchen, lounge, sitting room, family room, study, dining room and bathroom. In a household of eight souls it was always busy but never noisy. If the younger children were allowed a few precious minutes of childish games these were always conducted outside the house. If the weather was not suitably clement then it simply meant no playtime.

"Sorry my little ones," Aron would say, "Tis the will of God that there can be no play today. Sit down quietly and read your bible stories."

The three other rooms in the house were filled with a variety of cots and beds. One room accommodated the male children; a second was for the girls and the smallest room was just large enough to contain Aron & Mary's ancient iron bedstead.

Apart from the Sunday visits to Church, Aron only visited the local village at market time when he had sheep and lambs to sell. Mary would accompany him and after the business was concluded they would stock up with whatever non-perishable food stuffs and other commodities they required from the local store.

Both Aron and Mary could read and write and were careful to ensure that the children up to the age of sixteen always attended diligently to their school homework. Newspapers and magazines were strictly banned except for the local Diocesan newssheet. On one occasion Alan had smuggled a comic paper into the house and this had resulted in him being roundly thrashed by his father when the publication was discovered under his mattress. Apart from the Holy Bible only 'good books' were to be allowed; and that meant religious books and educational books. Some classic novels such as Dickens, Austen and Bronte passed the censor but only after careful perusal by Aron.

Sunday lunch was a special time in the Allbarrows household. It was the only day in the week when they always ate meat or poultry. Moreover, in honour of the Sabbath, Joseph and Alan, the two oldest sons were allowed to share a bottle of Guinness to wash down their meal and the younger ones were indulged with the treat of a bottle of 'White Lemonade.' Aron, as the good Catholic that he was, always said Grace before and after every meal. Apart from their excessive piety there were a number of other strange matters that distinguished the Allbarrows from their neighbours.

Before the Grace after Meals was recited Aron would always say,

"Now children, all together let us say the special little Allbarrow prayer, *NBAREK* And all the children would say in unison, *NBAREK*."

There was always one child present who would say,

"Dad, what is *NBAREK*? What does it mean?" and the only answer they ever got was,

"To be sure it's holy and in our family it has always been said." And that was the end of the matter until the next time the question was posed.

Then there was the matter of the candles. Everyone in church lit a candle, and sometimes their school friends told the children that they used candles on the dining table. But this was quite different to the way that Mary always had to light a pair of candles on Friday night and to wave her hands over them.

"To be sure it's a family tradition," Mary would answer when questioned about this strange ceremony. "Both among the Allbarrows and my own people the Meadows on the Waterford road, the Mother of the house always lights candles on a Friday night."

There was one other matter that had made generations of Allbarrow children curious and that was the question of the ancient flagstones behind the house. Aron and Mary's family were no different to their forebears and you could be sure that as each child reached the age of curiosity they would enquire,

"Mum or Dad (as the case might be), what are those strange markings on the middle flag stone at the end of the back garden?"

To call the rock strewn, overgrown area that lay behind the house a garden, might have been the Allbarrow's one and only pretension but the back garden was how it had always been described and probably always would be.

There were five of these ancient looking paving stones and four of them were unmarked. The fifth and centre one, however, was heavily engraved. With the passage of time in that often wet and windy corner of the world the markings had all but worn away. However, the children could still make out square box-like shapes, long thin lines like arrows and squiggles. Most Allbarrow children of the nineteenth and twentieth century had suspected that they were Egyptian hieroglyphics. There was a book about ancient Egypt in the house but the illustrations of the ancient script bore little or no similarity to the flagstone markings.

Succeeding generations of Allbarrow fathers always discouraged too much investigation.

"These stones are holy," Aron told Joseph, as his father had told him and his had told him, for as far back as anyone could remember.

"If anyone was to disturb them stones," he continued with a terrified look on his face, "You can be sure the wrath of Jaisus and the Almighty would be upon us all."

It was accepted practice throughout the generations that the first-born son of the Allbarrows would always inherit the stone cottage. The younger boys, when old enough to earn a living, would settle either in Ballymagee or in other small cottages in the area if they wished to pursue the family tradition of raising sheep. The girls too, with the exception of the oldest, would be married off to suitable young men once they reached the appropriate age. They would settle usually within a maximum of ten or twelve miles of the original Allbarrow home.

The only other family in the area who followed exactly the same traditions was the Meadows family. Their cottage was just six miles east of the Allbarrows' home on the old footpath that originally led in the general direction of

Waterford. To the best of Aron's knowledge, however, no Allbarrow or Meadows had ever set foot in that large and undoubtedly sinful town.

The same arrangement applied in reverse with the oldest son of the Meadows. He always inherited their stone cottage.

Historically, the two families always had a fairly high birth rate and as a result many of the residents of the local villages and surrounding farms had the same surnames of Allbarrow and Meadows. However, once the offspring from the two family homes flew the nest they were instructed, with the fear of heaven, never again to say *NBAREK* at the Sunday lunch nor to light candles on a Friday evening.

"Those things," the Father would say, "are special and just for the old family home. Our Lord does not want them to happen anywhere else."

Throughout the long and turbulent history of Ireland the population of that poor country had kept fairly constant. Mass emigration and frequent famine had ensured this. With each flood of poor Irish peasants setting out for England, America or Australia among the O'Flanagans, the O'Briens, the O'Reillys and the O'Flahertys there would always be a member of the Allbarrow or Meadows clan anxious to make a new home in a more hospitable land. These were, however, at least three generations removed from their forebears who had occupied one of the two family homes as children.

The one solid base on which all the family traditions were built was that the eldest son never left home. He inherited the house and always married a second cousin with pure Allbarrow or Meadows blood in her maternal line. This arrangement kept the family strictly in control. Moreover, with first cousins never permitted to marry, this rule helped to reduce the genetic risks of too much inbreeding. As a result, other than an inclination towards stubborn fanaticism that seemed to grow with every succeeding generation, the two families continued to breed children who were for the most part healthy in mind and body.

CHAPTER THREE

EXPULSION

SPAIN 1492

On the first of March 1492 Ferdinand and Isabella signed the dreaded decree. There had been nearly half a million Jews in Spain but of this number two thirds either before the edict or immediately afterwards, decided to convert to the dominant faith and thus ensure their future in their native country. The remainder, Jose and Rebecca and their three children among them, set out to find a new home in a more tolerant and hospitable land.

As the elegant carriage drove majestically out of the town the road quickly filled with hundreds of their fellow Jews all making their way westwards. They saw friends, relatives, employees, and poor labourers, rich artisans and merchants. There were doctors, Rabbis, philosophers, lawyers, poets, musicians, some with handcarts, some with backpacks, and a few in a variety of horse and donkey powered conveyances. Most of them, like the Alvaro family, knew that their ancestors had arrived in Spain long before the Visigoths and the Moors. But Ferdinand and Isabella had given them but three bitter choices. The choices were conversion, exile or death.

Turning for a last look at his beloved Cordoba, Jose could see vast crowds standing around the city walls watching their departure. He knew that among these people were many of his own relatives who had accepted baptism and the cross rather than the terrors of exile. He understood their feelings and thanked God for giving him and his family the strength to cling to the ancient faith of Abraham and Moses.

Jose had decided to make for the port of Cadiz. He knew that many of his co-religionists were heading for Portugal but he suspected that within a few years Portugal would follow the example of its neighbour Spain and expel the Jews. From Cadiz, where Jose had many business friends among the rich Christian ship owners, he felt certain he could charter a boat to North Africa

The journey from Cordoba to Cadiz was not overly long. In the comfort of their carriage, even after the winter rains, they could normally make good speed. However, today the road was clogged with his fellow Jews and at least as far as Seville Jose knew the going would be hard and slow. From Seville most of the refugees would take the northwest route into Portugal, he explained to Rebecca. And then they would be able to travel much faster.

They were only five miles out of Cordoba when Jose spied the figure of Rabbi Yair ben Moshe and his elderly wife pushing a small cart on which rested a Sepher Torah (scroll of the law) together with a few canvas bags obviously containing their personal possessions.

Jose was deeply distressed and realised that he had been so busy arranging his own departure that he had given little or no thought to those less able than himself. Quickly he reined in the horses and jumped from the carriage.

"Rav Yair," he addressed the old gentleman, "I am heart broken to see you in this situation. This is no place for a Sepher Torah or for a great scholar such as you. Where are you making for?"

"I have been invited to go to Cairo to study the texts of Maimonides," the Rabbi replied. "The messenger from Rav Ya'acov only arrived a month ago. I thank the Almighty for showing me an answer to my prayers. I wish all these other poor souls were as fortunate as me in having a new home waiting to welcome them."

Jose looked at the saintly old man in astonishment. He was already stained and exhausted from the journey. He was undergoing what would have been a great ordeal for a man half his age. And here he was thanking God for his good fortune.

"Please do me the honour of allowing me to convey you, your wife and your holy baggage to the port of Cadiz," Jose said. "From there we hope to take a ship to the Maghreb. I will instruct the Captain to then take you on to Cairo."

"You too," the Rabbi replied," are an instrument of the Almighty and I thank you for all your kindness. I pray that your good deeds will go before you and that the Lord will bless you in all you undertake."

"Thank you for the blessing," Jose answered, "Aharon! please help me load the Rabbi's belongings and ask the ladies to make room inside for both he and his wife."

Aharon was José's first-born son, a kind, gentle and sensitive young man who needed no encouragement to have the honour of assisting the Rabbi, his wife and belongings into the coach.

Soon they were on their way again but only two miles further on Jose saw his cousin, Sarah, six months pregnant, standing at the side of the road. She and her husband Yitzchak Mendoza together with their ten-year old daughter, Leah, were gazing in horror at the broken axle of their handcart and their belongings, strewn at the side of the road. Once again Jose stopped the carriage and quickly set about rescuing his kinsmen from their terrifying predicament. The carriage was now so full that the younger passengers were forced to sit on top of baggage.

Aharon who was sixteen years old sat alongside his father, taking his turn in guiding and reining their horse on its obstacle course of a journey. Yitzchak too sat aloft keeping a careful eye on the pile of wooden cases and cloth bundles that were the property of the passengers in this over laden vehicle.

In the afternoon the Rabbi had gently suggested to Jose that they should stop to recite Mincha, the afternoon prayer. When they did so, the male pedestrians quickly joined them. All were anxious to obtain the protection of the Almighty for their journey into the unknown.

That first evening the weather was kind and warm and they struck camp under some trees at the side of the road. They were not short of food thanks to the careful planning of Jose in anticipating this sad journey. And after dinner they recited the evening prayer, Arbit, together.

"Tomorrow will be a long and hard day," Jose told his fellow travellers after the service was over. "I strongly suggest that we all get as much sleep as we can, while we can, as who knows what problems lie in front of us tomorrow."

The Rabbi and his wife slept in the carriage to guard the Sepher Torah, the Law Scroll, while the rest of the party tried to sleep away the long dark hours under the stars. Jose lay alongside Rebecca and kissing her gently he turned over and closed his eyes. But sleep would not come. The previous night he had slept in his huge wooden framed bed in his beautiful bedroom surrounded by all the familiar luxuries he had always taken for granted. Now he was on his way into exile. But then, he mused, unless we Jews are living in the land of Israel we are always in exile. We are simply exchanging one exile for another. He had, however, never even considered returning to the ancient land from which his ancestor Aharon ben Yosef had fled nearly fifteen hundred years earlier. There were two men of his acquaintance who had made the dangerous pilgrimage some years ago. One had stayed and settled in a town called Safed in the north of the Galilee. The other had returned with reports of the appalling poverty afflicting the handful of Jews living in Jerusalem, Tiberias and Safed. The country was controlled by the Muslims but the lot of the Arabs, who were also forced to exist in filth and squalor, was virtually indistinguishable from that of the Jews

Rebecca was lying besides him on a sheet of bedding fabric. She was, of course, wearing her day clothes; a beautiful, full-skirted gown of silk as befitted the wife of a wealthy Spanish merchant. In the privacy of the glade that Jose had selected for his wife and for himself, Rebecca had uncovered her long, dark and shiny hair. Her delicate pale skin was always protected from the strong Spanish sun and she lay there looking so beautiful and so vulnerable that it broke José's heart to realise the extent to which his beloved Rebecca's life had suddenly changed. Jose studied her and realised that such a delicate flower could never have survived in the land of Israel as it had then become.

No, he thought, Italy or maybe the Maghreb (North Africa) is the place for us.

Jose himself was a tall handsome man with flashing dark eyes. His black hair was just beginning to show the first signs of greying at the temples. This was the only indication that this fine, youthful man was over, rather than under, forty years of age.

Jose dressed in the manner of his Christian neighbours and associates, except for the long rectangular robe he placed over his other clothing during the Sabbath and festivals. This garment, as required by Jewish law, had special fringes called Tsitsit at each of its four corners. Without this robe he could and frequently did pass as a Christian when travelling outside his native city. The only other distinguishing feature of his clothing was the traditional soft fabric Spanish cap that never left his head when he was outside his home. Many

Christians of the time also wore caps like that of Jose but for him covering the head was a Jewish religious precept. In the house and Synagogue a large black skullcap again in accordance with Jewish custom, replaced the cap.

Jose had been married to Rebecca for almost eighteen years and the love and respect they accorded to each other had ensured a strong happy marriage. They had produced three children. Aharon the first-born was sixteen and almost a young replica of his father from whom he had inherited a warm, caring nature. He idolised Jose and only wished to replicate his approach to life. Miriam their daughter was fourteen and had inherited her mother's beauty. Sadly she did not seem to have inherited her personality and was quick tempered and intolerant in her approach to others. She was particularly unpleasant to her younger brother, Elazar. She treated with him with consistent disdain. Fortunately Elazar had a champion in his big brother Aharon who always protected him from Miriam's frequent outbursts. Elazar was a shy introspective youth of twelve years. Academically he was average where Aharon at that age had already shown signs of high intelligence. However Elazar excelled in practical matters and had the ability to construct, design or repair almost any item quickly and efficiently.

Eventually Jose drifted off into a fitful sleep. He awoke soon after dawn to the sounds of movement emanating from inside the carriage. Rising, he quickly investigated and discovered Rabbi Yair preparing the Scroll of Law for the morning service. Somehow the Rabbi had managed to construct a waist high reading desk out of items of baggage and had placed the scroll on this steady but makeshift table. How the old man had managed to manhandle the heavy items without assistance filled Jose with horror.

"Come, Yosef," the Rabbi said using José's Hebrew name, "It is Thursday and we must read a portion of the Torah. Can you organise a Minyan, a quorum, of ten men so that we may commence our morning prayers?"

There were four men in José's own party and approaching the edge of the road he could see any number of candidates for their little congregation. Many of the Jewish exiles had trudged on through the night and they were indeed a sorry sight to behold. However as soon as Jose called out the seemingly magic word *Minyan* all those in earshot turned from the road and ran eagerly over to him to join in the prayers. Somehow the prayers that day had more meaning than they ever had before, to those assembled.

'Praise the Lord and His Holy Name,' 'Bless the Lord God of Israel for Ever and Ever,' 'The Lord of Hosts is with us,' ' Give us strength to return to Zion in mercy,' ' Let the Great Trumpet be sounded to announce our Freedom.'

Jews all over the world recited those words every day but circumstances had brought a new intensity to their meaning that day. Incredibly, by the time the prayers ended there were nearly three hundred people in the strange assembly in that wooded glade.

"My dear friends," Rabbi Yair called to them. His voice was normally weak and even in the confines of his small Synagogue in Cordoba; he was often difficult to hear. Today, miraculously, he was granted extra strength so that everyone present heard his few well-chosen words.

"Go in Peace and may the Almighty watch over us all as he watched over our ancestors when they came out of Egypt and Babylon. May He lead us all to good new lands where we can settle and prosper always awaiting the final redemption in the days of the Messiah."

Silently the people, many overcome with emotion, began to disperse to recommence their journeys. For the vast majority the long trudge westwards continued. Only the fortunate few had the benefit of being able to ride.

Jose and Aharon helped the Rabbi to stow the items of baggage that they had used as a makeshift table, back onto the top of the carriage. While this was taking place young Elazar sat on the stump of an old tree carefully guarding the scroll of the law, the Sepher Torah, which he rested lovingly upon his knee. This Sepher Torah was the most ancient in the whole of Spain. It had been brought to Cordoba over five hundred years earlier from the famous Talmudic College of Sura in Babylonia and was consequently known all over the Jewish world as the Sura Sepher. The parchment on which the holy Torah was inscribed was yellow with age but the *Sofrim,* (scribes) of Cordoba had ensured that every letter of every word was frequently inspected and maintained in a perfect state of clarity and accuracy. Had just one blemish or mistake been discovered, the scroll would have been rendered *Pasul* and unfit to be used, at least until the problem was rectified.

The parchment was rolled on to two staves that were themselves slotted into a large heavy wooden casing. When closed the casing was a perfectly circular drum shape and this opened into two hinged halves for reading.

The exterior of the casing was completely covered with Gold and Silver filigree work. There were those who said that this casing was even older than the scroll itself and had survived from a distant time when Jews were fleeing eastwards and had taken the Sepher from Judea to the academy at Sura for safe keeping. It must be emphasised that although it was clearly chronicled that the Sura Sepher had come to Spain in the year 986 from Babylonia, the story of the older origin of its casing could not be confirmed.

For the two remaining days of that first week Jose and his companions made reasonably good progress towards Cadiz, their ultimate goal. On the Friday afternoon they easily found a clearing near to the road where they could stop to spend the Sabbath. It was, of course, forbidden for them to travel between dusk on Friday and nightfall on Saturday and they knew they could not expect the protection of the Lord if they broke his commandment to keep the Sabbath day holy. They passed the time in prayer, rest and anticipation of what lay ahead.

Throughout all the time since they had left Cordova the early March weather had been very kind and they felt that this was a good indication that the Almighty was really with them.

Early the following week the trail divided and many of the other exiles took the north-western route towards central Portugal. Happily José's party was now on a wider and less congested road and they were grateful that they could make much faster headway towards Cadiz. Each night they were able to stop in a sheltered spot near fresh water and good pasture for the horses. They were able to bathe and change their clothes in the privacy of the trees and to wash their soiled garments so that they would dry over night in the warm air.

This would be the final night of their journey. They were now but half a day from Cadiz and the occasional ponds and streams with their attendant vegetation had given way to a sandy desert-like terrain. They all agreed that with Cadiz so near the previous facilities they had found at their nightly resting-places were no longer important. Emergency rations for the horses were needed for the first time and these were quickly unloaded from the rear of the coach. After eating from their own now depleted stock of food they settled down on the somewhat sandy bedding for the last night.

Jose was now quite used to sleeping under the stars and he slept deeply. He awoke with a start at about three o'clock to hear strange sounds coming from the coach. The Rabbi and his wife still slept there to guard the priceless ancient Sepher Torah, scroll of the Law. At first Jose thought he had imagined the noises but there was no doubt something was terribly wrong. There were sounds of scuffling followed by the muffled noise of running feet in the sand. Jose jumped up, grabbed his sword and broke into a run. As he approached he could hear the Rabbi weakly calling out for help. Jose yelled to Aharon and Yitzhak to follow him. He could now make out in the moonlight the figures of two men running away from the coach. They seemed to be carrying bundles of baggage and Jose could see that they were armed with scimitars.

"Look after the Rabbi," Jose called to Aharon. "Yitzhak, come with me."

As they pursued the thieves the path was strewn with the coach passengers clothing which the robbers dropped as they endeavoured to make good their escape.

Jose was convinced that they had got away with very little and eventually they gave up the chase. As they returned panting to the others they retrieved the stolen belongings littering the path. As they neared the camp they could see that everyone was now awake. Jose could not understand why they all seemed to be standing so still in a half circle around the coach.

They were only a few yards away from the camp when young Elazar saw them and ran towards them. He was sobbing inconsolably.

Jose held open his arms to his younger son and said,

"Elazar, whatever is the matter?"

Eventually the boy managed to blurt out,

"They have killed Rabbi Yair."

Jose dashed up to the coach to see the venerable old Rabbi lying on his back on the floor of the coach with his head hanging out of the open door, mouth wide open, eyes staring unblinkingly, like a discarded rag doll. His two arms were wrapped around the Sepher Torah. It was obvious that the two thieves had spotted the Scroll, with all its silver & gold adornments and only the incredible bravery of the Rabbi had stopped them from stealing it. He had paid with his life for his success in foiling their attempt.

"Aharon," Jose muttered, rears welling up in his eyes, "lift the Torah scroll off the Rabbi and place it on the seat of the coach."

It took much of Aharon's not inconsiderable strength to prise the scroll away from the Rabbi's deathly grip. He knew it must be done but somehow to separate the holy man from the object for which he had given his life made Aharon feel like a ghoulish grave robber himself.

As soon as the scroll, complete with its cloak and silver adornments, was safely on the coach seat Jose, now almost blinded by tears, lifted the frail body of the elderly Rabbi from the coach. He placed him on a sheet on the ground and gently closed the eyes that for so long had feasted on the writings of countless generations of those who had gone before him. He then covered the body with a second sheet and recited the special prayers prescribed for those who had just passed away.

Jose and Rebecca tried to comfort the Rabbi's widow who was totally inconsolable in her grief. She was also deeply traumatised as a result of the violence she had just witnessed and it took Rebecca some time to persuade the old lady to come away from where her husband lay so that the sage's body could be prepared for burial. A grave was dug at the side of the road although the entire group was deeply troubled that they were unable to give the Rabbi a more suitable resting-place.

By this time a large crowd of other Jews had gathered and the amazing story of how the Rabbi had saved the Sepher Torah was whispered throughout the gathering.

Jose gave the eulogy reminding all present,

"He lived by the Torah and he died protecting it."

Young Elazar prised a panel from the side of the coach and carefully carved his father's final words from the eulogy upon it.

Our Teacher Rabbi Yair ben Moshe
May his memory be a blessing and an inspiration for us and for all future generations.

It was probably the last Jewish funeral to take place in Spain for many hundreds of years.

Chapter Four

The San Fernando

Cadiz 1492

The unusually warm and dry spell of weather had broken. The coach containing Jose and his party was once again making much slower progress. Before it was the endless mass of tortured humanity trudging towards a new life. Now it was driving rain that quickly restored the road to Cadiz into the sea of mud from which it had just escaped. Still their destination was but a few miles from their last night's encampment and despite the slow progress it was only some three hours before Elazar spotted the sea in the distance. A chill wind was blowing, as they approached and the surface of the water, usually so calm and smooth was broken by large white-topped waves. Soon they were in the town and making their way to the portside office of Don Miguel, a rich Christian ship owner and an old friend and business colleague of Jose.

His own office was unoccupied but a clerk pointed out a large sailing vessel, the San Fernando and told Jose that he would find Don Miguel on board. Leaving the rest of his party sitting in the coach that had been their only home for far too long, Jose strode across the open quayside to where the San Fernando was moored. A surly sailor directed Jose to the ship's wardroom where he found his friend deep in conversation with the vessel's Captain.

As soon as he entered the room Don Miguel's face broke into a broad smile. He was obviously delighted to see his friend so unexpectedly.

"This is Alfonso the Captain," he told Jose.

"Now my dear Don Jose," Don Miguel continued his arm around José's shoulder. "Come and sit down, sip a glass of wine and tell me for what do I owe the pleasure of this visit."

"Maybe you have a special shipment of cargo?"

"Alas, old friend," Jose replied, "The cargo is my wife, my family, my friends and I. There are nine of us and we urgently need passage to either North Africa or Italy."

A look of puzzled consternation came over the face of Don Miguel. "It sounds as if you are leaving the country for good, my friend."

"Surely not," he continued. "Spain needs men of your calibre to build up the country now that Ferdinand and Isabella have finally vanquished the cursed Moor."

"Don Miguel," Jose replied quietly, "Don't you know we are Jews? Their Catholic Majesties have decreed that all Jews who will not convert to Christianity must leave Spain at once."

"Oh, come on, Jose," Don Miguel countered, "Surely their Majesties don't mean people like you. You're as Spanish as I am. Maybe they want to expel some of the poor Jews who have lived too long with the Moors and have grown like them; but not men of your wealth, breeding and capability."

"I thank you for those fine words," Jose replied, "but the edict says clearly and unequivocally that all Jews who refuse the Cross must leave at once or die."

"So there you have it," the ship owner answered, "Convert! You'll still worship God but just in a different way. I know lots of Jewish families who have converted over the last few generations. Why some of them have produced Priests and even a couple of Bishops."

"I also know many families of Conversos," Jose countered sadly, "And I know how many of them have been interrogated by the Inquisition. Then they are tortured and murdered and all in the name of the Jewish carpenter from Nazareth."

Don Miguel was an honest, God-fearing man and he looked carefully at the face of his friend and long-time associate. He saw that further argument would be pointless.

Suddenly he began to feel angry. So this is the future for our beloved country, he pondered. We cursed the Moor for his intolerance and now we are behaving the same way ourselves.

"God help Spain," he exclaimed, "if she is driving out such as you."

"This ship, the San Fernando, is sailing to Casablanca tomorrow."

Suddenly they both realised that Captain Alfonso had been standing behind them, near the door, during the entire conversation. He was a sullen, swarthy man and looked as if he had far too large an appetite for both food and strong drink. During the conversation his face had become increasingly contorted with rage and anticipating the question he was about to be asked, he blurted out,

"Don, Miguel. You know that this is supposed to be a shipment of cargo only."

"You have always refused to take passengers. We have only a small crew and I can't take responsibility for the Jews."

Don Miguel could hardly believe his ears. He had never liked Alfonso but he did his job well enough and he kept the motley crew of sailors in order. Moreover, he had always previously addressed Don Miguel with a mealy-mouthed deference.

"How dare you," the Ship owner thundered, "These people are my friends and will be treated as honoured guests on any ship of mine. You are taking them and that is that."

Don Miguel turned to Jose. "How many rooms will you need for your party?"

"Seven would be ideal but we could manage very well with just five," Jose replied quietly.

"This ship has eight cabins and contrary to what you have just heard, we have often taken fare-paying passengers. I really do not know what has got into Captain Alfonso."

He had now regained his composure and the ship owner rounded on the Captain and coldly instructed him to prepare seven cabins.

Alfonso, even angrier than before, did not trust himself to speak. He turned on his heel, wrenched open the door and marched out defiantly, without uttering a single word.

"Oh dear," said Jose, "I'm so sorry that I have been the cause of your Captain becoming so upset. I know that good men are hard to find."

"Don't worry, Jose," his friend replied, "He'll get over it and I'm sure he will be glad to have the company of intelligent, educated people on the voyage."

Jose glanced at his friends face to ascertain if he really believed the last statement himself and being convinced it was only said to make him feel a little easier he quickly closed the subject of the Captain. However, deep in their hearts both men knew that Alfonso could prove to be a problem but little did they know to what extent their private fears would be justified?

"Now Don Miguel," Jose continued, "Please let me know the price for the voyage to Casablanca. I must make arrangements for payment today. I take it that Gold coins would be acceptable?"

A surprisingly modest sum was suggested by Don Miguel and agreed gratefully by Jose.

When the Jewish merchant tried to express his appreciation for the help and generosity the retort from the Christian ship owner was,

"I have lost count of the numerous occasions when you helped me to solve problems with my ships at foreign ports. I can never repay your many acts of kindness to me. If I thought you would allow it I would take no payment from you. But I know you too well to suggest that. We are Spaniards, Jew and Christian and Spaniards are a proud people."

They embraced as Don Miguel muttered in an emotion choked voice,

"Vaya con Dios, my friend, may God go with you."

Jose returned to the coach to find the passengers, with the exception of the Rabbi's widow, strolling up and down near the conveyance.

"We are sailing tomorrow for Casablanca," he announced.

The afternoon passed quickly with the gold coins being delivered to the strong room of Don Miguel and all the parties" baggage being loaded onto the vessel.

Once all were safely installed on board Jose went off to dispose of the coach and horses.

The Captain was nowhere to be seen while all this transpired and the first mate, a converted Jew by the name of Manuel and two ratings helped them to settle in with all their possessions.

The old lady, the Rabbi's widow was allocated a small cabin on her own. It was only just over twenty-four hours since the violent death of her husband and she immediately started to prepare to mourn him in accordance with Jewish custom. She seated herself on the hard floor of the cabin and as soon as the other members of the party had stowed away their belongings they each made their way to her cabin to try and comfort her in her grief.

Jose, meanwhile, as soon as the horses and carriage were sold had set off to inform the local militia of the murder of the Rabbi and the attempted robbery that had occasioned the tragic happening. The Sergeant, a good man, listened sympathetically and noted down the description of the two scoundrels. He promised Jose that he and his men would do everything possible to apprehend the murderers.

As a government official he was of course well aware of the expulsion order recently promulgated against the Jews by Ferdinand and Isabella.

"What are you going to do Don Jose?" he enquired sympathetically. "I know you are a Jew but to me you will always be one of the finest Spanish Gentlemen I have ever had the privilege to know."

Jose gave the Sergeant a searching look. Most of the militiamen were ignorant, illiterate peasants, rabidly anti-Jewish and anti-Muslim. They were fed a constant stream of hatred and prejudice by the priests who preached incessantly against the corrupting influences of the infidels on the sanctity of Holy Spain. As a consequence they were delighted to carry out the requirements of the new edict in as cruel and unpleasant a manner as possible. There were just a handful of genuine lawmen, such as this sergeant among the officers and although they did their best to restrain the worst excesses of the rabble they led, they were fighting a losing battle.

"Thank you for the enquiry," Jose replied, "Alas, we must leave Spain. We are sailing tomorrow."

The sergeant gave Jose a courtly bow and repeated the words of Don Miguel,

"Vaya con Dios, Don Jose. May God go with you."

The route from the militia offices back to the port took Jose passed the Cathedral and as he strode by, Jose was intrigued to catch sight of Captain Alfonso entering the famous old church. From his previous encounter Jose found it impossible to imagine the Captain attending church, even on a Sunday, let alone on a weekday afternoon.

Sadly the reason for the Captains apparent piety became only too obvious the following morning as the ship glided gently away from its moorings to commence the voyage to North Africa.

Don Miguel had risen early and by half past five he was aboard saying a last goodbye to his old friend. At six o'clock he made his way down the gangplank and watched as it was pulled aboard. Jose and all his party, with the exception of the distraught elderly widow and Miriam who had returned to the cabin to collect a warm cloak, were on deck waving to the solitary figure of Don Miguel on the deserted quayside. Suddenly, with the ship only a few metres away from its mooring, an open horse-drawn trap came into view in the early morning sunshine. Jose watched curiously as the vehicle was reined to a halt just behind where Don Miguel was standing. Two militiamen and two priests jumped from the trap and approached Don Miguel. By now, the ship was some ninety metres from the dockside and it was impossible to hear what the men were saying to the Spanish ship owner.

At first Jose wondered whether the militia had apprehended the thieves who had murdered Rabbi Yair. That made no sense at all, he decided. Why bring two priests to impart such news. Then Jose saw that there appeared to be some altercation between Don Miguel and the new arrivals. The two militiamen seized Don Miguel by the arms and started to roughly escort him back to their conveyance. One of the priests took his position in front of the three men holding aloft a large cross. The other priest took his place behind the group as the strange procession made its way back to the trap. The ship was now well away from the quayside and Jose, although he knew he could not be heard, started to shout to the party on shore to release his friend instantly. The more he shouted the more incensed he became until this strong man who had borne so much, broke down with tears of impotent fury.

He turned to Rebecca and saw behind her the figure of Captain Alfonso, a broad smile of triumph upon his face.

"The Holy Inquisition will soon look after that Jew-loving traitor," he said with a leer, "This ship is now mine and you Jews are going to have to work your passage."

Jose was not a violent man. His usual weapon of persuasion was the tongue. Now he knew why Captain Alfonso had visited the Cathedral the previous afternoon and in his anger at what the captain had done, he lost all control. He hurled himself at the smirking Alfonso and with fist flaying he knocked him to the ground. Rebecca had never seen her husband in such a rage. Jose jumped on top of the Captain and started to beat him. The passengers and crew who were on deck at the time stood in startled amazement at the scene but now two sailors stepped forward and dragged Jose off their Captain.

Alfonso staggered to his feet no longer smirking. His nose and lip were gushing blood as he shouted,

"Fling him into the lockup."

Turning to Rebecca in her elegant gown he screeched, almost besides himself with rage,

"Get down on the floor Jew-bitch and clean the mess on this deck!"

Her daughter Miriam, normally difficult and argumentative knelt down besides her mother to help her.

"Not you," the Captain bawled, "I said HER! I've got other work for you. Get below decks the rest of you and await my instructions."

The Alvaro family was at sea in more ways than one.

Chapter Five

The New Recruit

Ballymagee 1990

As had been the custom for more generations than anyone could imagine, each morning saw the Allbarrow men arising at the crack of dawn to drive their flocks out to new pastures on different parts of McGillicuddys Reeks. The area was hilly and strewn with rocks and boulders. The tough grass that grew there on the lower slopes was only fit for sheep and goats and even that grazing quickly disappeared if one was foolhardy enough to climb above one hundred feet or so up the dark threatening hillsides. Aron, as was the practice in the area, divided the sheep into three flocks of roughly equal size. Joseph, Alan, the second son and Aron himself supervised these flocks and undertook each day to search out fresh grazing.

Joseph was a bright young man who had done well at the village school. The teachers were deeply sorry that Aron had removed him from their influence before he had completed his 'leaving' certificate. They knew only too well the attitude to education from most of the parents in those parts. The children would be sent out to work, of one kind or another, as soon as they were literate and numerate and/or had reached the earliest possible legal age to be withdrawn from school. Joseph had enjoyed school but he knew that to stay on was out of the question. He therefore accepted his scholastic fate without argument. He was, after all the first-born of the Allbarrows and he thought he knew where his responsibility to the family lay. He became a shepherd, just like his father and his grandfather and he tended his flock diligently.

By the time Alan had left school and taken his place alongside his father and older brother, Joseph was beginning to feel an increasing sense of frustration and dissatisfaction with his life. There can be no doubt that this was a direct result of his secret habit of taking a book with him each day to read as he sat on the rugged hillside. His father would have been horrified although the books that Joseph liked were nothing more sensational than school History and Geography textbooks.

The more he read about the great wide world the more a longing grew in him to travel. But he was the firstborn and that meant he must stay at home, tend the flocks, marry a second cousin from the Meadows clan and eventually inherit the old stone house. He felt trapped. He knew that a number of his old school friends from the village had left for Cork or even far away Dublin. It was whispered in the town that three of his former classmates were now in such exotic locations as London, Manchester and Birmingham. But all this was denied to the presumed heir to the Allbarrows.

In May 1990 the Irish Army set up their mobile recruitment office in the village. Joseph had been sent on one of the bicycles to buy some groceries at the store. As he passed the Army office with its attractive display of posters of smart young Irish men in uniform he paused to read the leaflets posted outside the prefabricated structure. As he read he was startled to hear a friendly voice from behind him.

"Why not come in and hear more about life in the Army, my lad," the voice intoned. "To be sure 'tis a grand life for a strong young man like yerself."

He turned to see the friendly smiling face of the recruiting sergeant.

Joseph shook his head. "No thank you, Sir," he replied, feeling guilty and embarrassed at having even stopped outside the cabin.

"I'm just on my way to get some messages and I'd best be getting on with it."

"Well come in next time you're in the village, lad," the recruiting Sergeant continued, "And in the meantime take this brochure with you to have a look at."

"Thank you, Sir, that I will," Joseph answered, carefully folding the booklet and placing it in his jacket pocket.

There was no way he could allow his parents or smaller siblings to see the brochure. For the firstborn of the Allbarrows to even dream of an army career would be a total betrayal of all his family traditions.

That night Joseph hardly slept. He tossed and he turned all the time aware that his restlessness might disturb his brother Alan who shared his bed. Whenever he did manage to drift off to sleep he awoke just minutes later from a recurring dream that had him overwhelmed with feelings of excitement and elation alternating with those of profound guilt. How could he, the eldest son of the Allbarrows, imagine himself far away in the Irish Army? In his dream he was smartly dressed in the same uniform as the sergeant he had spoken to that day. Indeed he wore the three stripes of a sergeant. Joseph dreamed that he was sitting at a pavement café staring out at crowds of passers by in a square surrounded by gleaming white buildings and bathed in sunshine much brighter than he had ever experienced, even in the midst of an Irish summer day.

When, mercifully, the time arrived to arise he dressed quickly and made sure that the army brochure was well out of sight, thrust deep inside his pocket. He said his morning prayers quickly, ate his breakfast and set off with his sheep dog and flock to the designated pasture for that day.

As soon as he was sure that the sheep were grazing contentedly he found a large rock and sat down to read the forbidden document. He was fascinated by what the leaflet told him and his own vivid imagination fleshed out what the brochure did not say.

Joseph saw himself training, drilling, learning and travelling all over the beautiful island on which he lived. He would see Dublin and Cork, Tipperary and Waterford, he decided. There would be danger patrolling the bandit country in the north by the Ulster border and where the troubles still rumbled on. He read that Irish troops often left the Emerald Isle to work with the United Nations abroad. He would travel far from these rocky hillsides as he had yearned to do since he first learned geography at school.

For most of that day he read and re-read that leaflet and he dreamed a thousand dreams. But deep down he knew they could only be dreams for him. He was a firstborn of the Allbarrows. However, the dreams were sweet, very sweet.

Six months went by and Joseph pushed all thoughts of joining the army to the back of his mind. He became quieter and more introspective; he ate less and smiled only occasionally. His parents noticed the change in him.

"I don't know what ails young Joseph," Mary whispered to Aron late one night as they lay on their hard mattress.

"Aren't you after thinking he's gone so quiet lately?"

"Now you come to mention it, so he has," Aron agreed. "He probably needs to be settling down with a nice woman and that'll cure him, to be sure."

"But the lad's not even quite nineteen yet," Mary pointed out, "You know as well as me that a lad must be twenty-one before he's wedded in our family."

"Well Joseph is advanced for his age, Aron replied. "He always was a bright lad."

"He'll be as right as rain," Aron continued, "Don't worry. Good night Mary!"

With that he turned over and fell into his usual deep sleep.

The following afternoon when Joseph returned with the flock his mother asked him to take a newly baked cake down to the church in the village for Father Meadows. As Joseph pedalled into town he saw that the army recruiting office had returned. He thought he had convinced himself to forget all thoughts of leaving home to join the army. However the sight of the portable building with its bright recruiting posters outside overturned his resolve and within minutes he found himself within the structure.

The sergeant in charge was not the same one as last time but he was equally friendly.

"Sit down, my lad," he invited, gesturing towards a chair in front of his desk.

As soon as he was seated Joseph began,

"I read the leaflet the last time you were here. Please would you be after telling me a little more about it all? Life in the army I mean," he finished lamely.

Joseph listened intently as the sergeant described life in the modern Irish army. The brochure had made it sound pretty good but what the soldier was now telling him sounded wonderful. Even the bad bits, the danger, the discomfort of living in makeshift billets on overseas postings for the UN, the discipline, the drilling; all this was music to Joseph's ears. He realised that life in the army surpassed even the best his own vivid imagination had been able to conjure up.

When the sergeant eventually finished Joseph stuttered,

"Thank you very much sir, I only wish I could join you."

"But you can my lad," the soldier answered, "All you need to do is to sign this paper and providing you pass your medical you're in."

Joseph felt obliged to explain about his parents and family and the traditions of the firstborn of the Allbarrows.

The sergeant told him his loyalty to his family and its traditions was praiseworthy but he must consider a higher loyalty to his country where bright, strong young men were desperately needed in the army.

Finally Joseph promised to discuss the matter with his parents.

He delivered the cake to the priest and set off back to the stone house with his head in a whirl. The recruitment office would only be in town until the end of the week so he must act at once.

That night, after all the younger children were in bed Joseph plucked up courage to tell his parents what he wanted to do. They were even more shocked and horrified than he had anticipated. He thought his father might fly into a rage as he used to do when Joseph was younger. Aron however was hurt, upset and puzzled. He knew from his own father that his great grandfather was the second son because the firstborn had run away but in all the family history that was the only time that such a terrible thing had happened. Now here he was facing just such a problem. He blamed himself. There must have been something in Joseph's upbringing that had been defective. Had he not explained the family traditions to his son properly? Had he in some way shown a lack of enthusiasm for the Friday candles or NBAREK, he pondered?

Mary began to weep. She was also concerned for the family tradition but as a mother the thought of her son facing danger from some terrorist on the northern border terrified her even more than the breaking of family tradition.

They tried every conceivable argument and form of persuasion but they could see that short of making him a prisoner in his own home they were losing the battle.

Joseph for his part was adamant and pointed out that Alan was only a year younger and would be only too happy to take over his mantle as the heir of the Allbarrows.

Finally Aron said,

"There is just one final thing we can do."

He explained to Joseph that according to family custom, whenever a serious crisis arose, they must go to the old flagstones at the end of the back garden and stand in front of the centre one with all the strange markings. There they must pray to God for guidance.

It was much too dark outside to find the slabs at night and so at the crack of dawn, after a sleepless night for father, mother and son the two men nervously made their way down the garden to the ancient stones.

As they approached the edge of the stone, Joseph prepared to kneel.

"No, my son," Aron said. "We are speaking here directly with God in his heaven and not through sweet Jaisus. The family custom is to stand with your head bowed to look upon the face of the stone."

Aron took a deep breath. "We the sons of the Allbarrows need your guidance dear Lord," he read from a yellowed piece of paper he extracted from his pocket.

"Young Joseph here wants to go off and join the army. He would be giving up his rights as the firstborn of the Allbarrows. His mother and I do not want him to go. Please give us a sign, oh Lord."

Father and son then lapsed into a deep silence punctuated only by the heavy breathing of Aron. They both stared intently at the flagstone expecting, so it seemed, that it would answer them in a human voice. The only voice they heard, however, came from within them. A feeling of peace swept over Joseph and he found himself ready to accept without resentment whatever his father would finally decide.

For Aron too the feelings of anger and disappointment gradually faded and the love that he felt for his son and indeed for all his children began to take primacy in his mind. He knew that the path that Joseph wished to take was a dangerous one. His radio news often reported the sad fate of an Irish soldier helping to maintain world peace in a distant land. He felt however, that if God was softening his heart, to let the boy go he would also protect him and bring him safely home again once Joseph had satisfied his longing to travel.

They had stood almost stationary for ten minutes seemingly oblivious to the cold, swirling mist that was gradually enveloping them. Looking down once more at the yellowed paper still clutched in his hand, Aron took four steps backwards, then he bowed to the right, bowed to the left and finally directly towards the flagstone.

Joseph who had watched this little ceremony carefully followed suit until he was standing once more shoulder-to-shoulder with his father.

At last Aron spoke, "My son," he intoned in a strange choked voice. "It is the will of the Almighty that you go from this place and join the army. May God protect you always."

Aron the strict seemingly cold father then took his son in his arms and they both wept copiously on each other's shoulders.

Then they dried their eyes and endeavoured to regain their composure before making their way back to the stone house.

Aron quickly told Mary the outcome of their prayers and she in turn broke down and wept. But all three of them knew with certainty that they were fulfilling the will of the Almighty and that His will must be accepted in joy.

Chapter Six

Captain Alfonso

At Sea-1492

It had been dull and overcast when the *San Fernando* had slipped out of Cadiz harbour. Now just half an hour after setting sail for North Africa the ship was doing battle with a vicious storm whose intensity was increasing by the minute. First the mariners had noticed a change in the wind's direction and the white topped, choppy waves breaking against the side of the vessel. Then as they approached midday the sky grew black and the wind increased in intensity until it seemed that it would tear the sails to shreds. Now the elements were hurling rain, sleet and hail against the ship. Huge waves were breaking over the bows. All the passengers and most of the crew were huddled below decks in their respective quarters as they listened in terror to the incessant noise resulting from the ferocity that nature had unleashed upon them.

Captain Alfonso however, still found time to instruct the female passengers to get down on their hands and knees to scrub the floors of the gangways, the cabins and the crews quarters, below decks. Two evil looking sailors were instructed to supervise this work and took delight in watching as one by one their charges succumbed to bouts of retching seasickness. These fiends found it hysterically amusing that the women were spoiling the results of their own labours by incessantly vomiting on the newly scrubbed floors. Rebecca pleaded with them to show a little mercy but they were true and trusted servants of their captain and they carried out his orders with uncommon zeal.

Jose was still in solitary confinement and lay in the rat-infested lockup in the pitch-blackness almost grateful for the noise of the storm as his only contact with the world outside. The other men of his party were put to work repairing damage to the ship, battening down moveable items of furniture and dragging heavy cases of cargo into safer locations in the hold. They too were feeling the worse for the weather but their taskmasters were no more sympathetic to their plight than their colleagues who were guarding the women. Even the elderly widow of Rabbi Yair was instructed to repair items of the crew's clothing that needed sewing and darning. Much of this was filthy and evil smelling but still traumatised by the sudden violent death of her husband, she hardly noticed her own predicament.

There was only one member of the party of passengers who was treated with even a vestige of respect and that was Miriam, José's and Rebecca's usually wayward daughter.

The captain had locked her up on her own in the best cabin. He had instructed, before the storm broke out, that she was to be fed with the finest provisions aboard; the ones usually reserved for his own table. She was supplied with water for bathing and her father's books were brought to her cabin to occupy her time. She was as much a prisoner as all the others but at least her cell lacked for no creature comforts. Nevertheless Miriam was furious to be locked up. She had no idea of the treatment being meted out to the others with the sole exception of her mother who she had last seen scrubbing the decks. She imagined that the captain had just wanted to frighten Rebecca and that by now she would be ensconced in her own cabin with her father, Jose.

Now the storm was raging and although her young constitution was quite capable of coping with the way the ship was rolling, she was becoming increasingly anxious to ascertain why she was being treated as a prisoner. Over night the weather hardly abated but Miriam still managed to sleep. A member of the crew awakened her early the following morning. He carefully unlocked and then re-locked the cabin door as he entered with her breakfast.

"How dare you come in here without knocking?" she enquired imperiously. But the evil looking fellow simply laughed, placed the tray on the table and left, carefully locking the door behind him.

She looked at the breakfast and could see straight away that the large plate contained meat. It looked like pig meat she decided and definitely not for consumption by a Jewess. She was very hungry but she could never bring herself to eat forbidden foods. Once again she became angry as she conjectured on what she would say to her father about the breakfast. He would be as horrified as she was and would certainly register a serious complaint with his friend Don Miguel. Miriam was blissfully unaware of the fate that had befallen that fine gentleman and had wondered why whatever the Captain had said to her father, as she had returned to the deck the previous day, had provoked such fury in response.

Miriam was soon reminded of her hunger and returning to the tray she managed to extract some dried fruit and raw vegetables. These she consumed quickly and having dressed in one of her favourite gowns she sat down to await release from her captivity. By now she had decided that the door was locked to protect her from the temptation to explore the ship during the storm and as a result of so doing, to fall and be injured during the frequent heaving of the wild sea.

She settled down to read for most of the morning until she decided that enough was enough and began to bang on the door of the cabin for someone to come and release her. This was to no avail and eventually she came to the conclusion that the continuing noise of the storm was drowning out all her attempts to be heard. She returned to her book until the same impertinent sailor unlocked the door and entered with her lunch. Miriam quickly glanced at the tray and was relieved to see that it was fish and therefore less likely to offend the dietary laws. However this time, she decided, this ruffian was not going to lock her in again.

"Thank you for lunch," she intoned casually in her best 'young mistress' voice, "You can leave the door open now as I will probably stretch my legs as soon as the weather quietens down."

This request seemed to amuse the scoundrel even more than her comment at breakfast and he left the cabin guffawing loudly as he locked her up once again.

Miriam hurled herself against the door and began to shout, scream and hammer all to no avail. Eventually she collapsed onto the floor in a flood of tears of rage until she remembered the fish and decided that her hunger was even more important than her freedom.

In the evening the door was again unlocked and this time Miriam was amazed to see that the captain himself had brought her meal.

"And how are you, my beauty?" he enquired with his eyes staring intently at her heaving bosom.

"I hope you are enjoying the voyage," he continued, "despite the terrible weather." And then putting out his filthy hand he had the impertinence to pat her on the cheek.

Suddenly and for the first time Miriam was frightened. A man like that would never have dared to touch her unless he felt he had her completely in his power.

"I would like to see my father," she responded with as much dignity as she could muster.

"Sorry my love," he replied, "Not possible. Your father is far too busy. However, if there is anything you want just ask me. I will be delighted to look after a pretty young lass like you."

"I must go now," he continued, with his voice suddenly becoming hoarse, "but as soon as the storm abates I'll come back and we can have some fun together."

Once again he leered at her and after longingly staring at her bosom for a few further seconds he turned abruptly and left the room. Miriam ran to the door in the vain hope that the captain had forgotten to lock it. She was disappointed. He would hardly let a prize catch, like her, go, she decided. The over-confident, arrogant, spoilt daughter of the Alvaro family was now terrified and sick to the stomach as she contemplated her fate at the hands of the evil captain.

Although she was deeply frightened she still had within her the fire and determination which until now had caused her nothing but trouble within her family circle. No, she thought, that disgusting creature is not going to get the better of me. She began to plot how she would get away from the clutches of Alfonso and a plan began to take shape within her active brain.

Miriam knew exactly what the captain had in mind and she began to search the cabin for some weapon with which she could defend herself. When her meals were delivered a knife was supplied and she had already noticed that the sailor who collected the tray after she had eaten always checked carefully to see that it was in place with her plate, mug and condiments when he collected the soiled pots. This night the captain had brought the food and there was no knife supplied. She would have to wait until breakfast, she decided.

The following morning she took the tray from the mariner as soon as he entered and waited for him to exit the cabin and to start to re-lock the door from the outside. She quickly grabbed the knife from the tray and hid it under her bed. By now she could hear the sound of the huge iron key being removed from the lock as she called out and started banging on the door. To her relief she heard him replace the key, unlock and open the door.

"Now what do yer want?" he scowled.

"You've not left me a knife," she responded, smiling as sweetly as she could at the man.

"I'm sure there was one there," he ventured and glancing down at the tray he muttered, "Oh well, maybe not, I'll go and get one now."

The sailor returned just moments later with another knife and Miriam knew her plan was going to work.

Leaving her breakfast aside she now set out to find the next item that she would need. This proved to be remarkably easy to locate. She had noticed a large chest in the corner of the cabin on which was piled some of her family's baggage. Swiftly she pulled the bundles and smaller wooden cases off the top of the chest and opened it. Much to her delight she saw that it contained a wide assortment of bottles of liquor. There was Brandy, Rum and a wide assortment of wines. She selected a bottle of the strongest Cognac and placed it under the bed with the newly acquired knife. She now had the two main elements she would need to defend herself against the lascivious designs of Captain Alfonso.

She sat down to eat her porridge; it was quite cold by now but she did not care. It was food and she ate it; she knew that she must keep up her strength for the task that lay ahead. While she had been busy formulating and preparing her simple plan she had not had time to consider the dangers associated with what she was setting out to achieve. Suddenly the enormity of the plan struck her and she began to wonder if there was any other option open to her. She pondered on this but could see no other way out. It was obvious to her from the attitude of the captain and crew that they must have her beloved father and all the rest of his party imprisoned. It seemed to her that there was little likelihood therefore, that any of them would be able to rescue her. It was all down to her. Miriam did not consider herself brave. She knew that something totally abhorrent was about to happen to her and she had to resist. It was as simple as that. A quiet gentle girl like her best friend Naomi would simply have wept and cowered away from someone like Captain Alfonso but Miriam was made of sterner stuff.

Still the storm raged on and most of the passengers and even members of the crew were constantly ill. Below decks with the sole exceptions of Miriam's cabin and the bare cell of Jose, the entire area stank with stale vomit. Men and women just lay down anywhere, floors, and bunks, under tables, their stomachs heaving in sympathy with the ship's gyrations.

On the third day the weather improved a little. Enough for Captain Alfonso, although exhausted, to hand over the bridge to the first mate, Manuel. He could not forget for a minute the beautiful young Jewess he was longing to de-flower. Storm or no storm, he could wait no longer. His desire must be satiated.

He entered Miriam's cabin, his clothes dripping wet from the huge waves still breaking over the bows of the ship. At first she thought it was a member of the crew arriving early with her meal but no, the moment she had been dreading had now arrived. Alfonso slowly and carefully closed and locked the door, slipping the huge key into a large pouch he always wore around his hips. Then he turned to look at her and without interrupting his stare even for a second; he quickly peeled off his soaking outer garments. These he allowed to drop in an untidy pile just in front of the door. A pool of water began to form round them as Miriam watched in horrified, fascinated silence.

Alfonso was a large swarthy man of probably fifty years. He wore a goatee beard in the Spanish style. The rough stubble of at least three days growth covered the rest of his face. He stripped down to a filthy chemise that at one time had probably been white and his pantaloons that strained to encase his huge stomach and then finally he spoke.

"I promised to come and see you my dear," he said in a voice that was hoarse with passion.

Miriam trembled as he crossed the room and seated himself in a large chair.

"Come near me, my child," he uttered, "So I can see you properly."

"Ain't you a pretty young lady, to be sure?" he leered.

Finding inner reserves of courage Miriam at last spoke. She was sure that her voice was quivering with fear but she tried her best to sound as friendly as possible.

"Captain," she said, forcing a brittle smile on to her face, "You have been so long on the bridge you must be exhausted. I found a bottle of my father's best cognac and hid it under the bed for you."

She quickly crossed the room and feeling his eyes following her every move she carefully bent down to retrieve the bottle from under the bed. At the same time she gently pushed the knife up to wall where it could be reached from the far side of the bed. She had practised both planting and retrieving the knife many times to ensure it would be where she needed it, when she needed it.

As soon as the Captain saw the bottle in her hand he smacked his lips.

"That's my girl," he said, "First pour me a nice drink and then come and sit here." He patted his huge fat thighs and again leered at the young girl.

Miriam poured a large brandy and forced herself to sit on his lap. The drink was downed at one gulp and Miriam immediately arose to pour him another. Again he made her sit and again he downed the Cognac in one gulp. This process was repeated no less than seven times after which he hurled the crystal glass across the room where it shattered all over his outer clothing by the door.

"That'ch enough," he said, his speech now quite slurred as a result of the large amount of liquor he had just consumed.

"Let's get these cursed clothes off you and get down to business, my pretty one."

He started to fumble with the hooks on the back of her dress.

"I'll do it," she said, glad of any excuse to rise and put a little distance between them.

"You come over to the bed and lie down there to watch me. You'd like that, wouldn't you?" she asked him, trying to sound as provocative as possible.

Alfonso, however, proved incapable of arising from the chair without assistance or for that matter walking across the room to the bed and Miriam was forced to assist him.

He eventually sat on the bed and immediately collapsed onto his back.

Turning his face towards her he growled,

"Well, ger on with it then. Let's have a look at what you are hiding under there."

Careful to keep just out of reach, Miriam slowly undid the hooks of her gown and allowed it to drop to the floor. Then she stepped back to pick up the beautiful garment and carefully placed it on the newly vacated chair. She was now wearing just a bodice and pantaloons.

"Come on, Come on," the captain mumbled. "What about the rest of it?"

"It would be better if you did that," Miriam was astounded to hear her own voice replying.

Slowly she walked up to the bed hoping that she was successfully concealing the feelings of revulsion and nausea that she was now experiencing. Then she climbed on top of the disgusting man straddling his mountainous stomach with her legs. She knew she must now bend forward and put her soft young face against his rough cheek. As she did so, she felt his right arm slowly encircling her small waist. Her right arm dropped down the side of the bed by the wall until she felt the knife handle in her hand. She pulled herself up with a jerk, her hand holding the knife hidden by the sheets. As she did so she heard him mumble incoherently and she felt the grasp of his arm on her waist loosening.

"I'm going to take off my bodice now," she whispered alluringly, "but you must look over towards the door while I undress. When you look back you will get a lovely surprise."

"Yesh, yesh," the captain smirked, a foul odour escaping from his mouth.

"Well go on then," Miriam continued, "Look over towards the door."

The captain turned his head and the beginnings of a shout began to form in his mouth. However, the flow of blood from between his lips quickly cut off the sound as Miriam plunged the knife over and over again into the chest of the evil man. Then with a last shudder the captain was dead.

Miriam jumped off the inert figure and realised she was covered in blood. She felt sick and very frightened as the enormity of what she had done, began to sink in. However, she knew what she had to do next. The fact that she was wearing only blood stained undergarments was of no importance. She must find her father and the others.

Taking the bunch of keys from the dead captain's pouch she silently unlocked the door of her cabin. The gangway outside was empty and shaking with fear and cold she crept along it. At the end was another gangway and peeping round the corner she saw her brother Aharon repairing broken floor timbers. Satisfied that he was alone she gently called to him. Aharon looked up and immediately saw the face of his sister peeping round the corner. She beckoned him to follow her and they returned to the cabin where she quickly locked the door

Aharon took in the situation at a glance. The blood stained body of the captain on the bed and the condition of his sister said it all.

"Miriam, oh Miriam, what happened? Are you hurt?" he said, holding out his arms to embrace and comfort her.

"I'm fine," she lied, "But we are still in great danger."

"I know that," Aharon replied, "But what did happen? How did you kill the monster?"

"Please Aharon," Miriam replied, "I am terrified we will be caught by members of crew and that will really be the end of us. Stop asking questions. I'll tell you the whole story later. Where are the others?"

Before Aharon could reply they heard approaching footsteps. He quickly dashed over to the bed and with a great tug pulled the knife from the chest of the late unlamented Alfonso. Hiding behind the door, knife at the ready, he signalled to Miriam to call for help as the sailor sauntered by. He heard her cry, unlocked the door with his own key and stepped into the cabin. He took one look at Miriam in her blood stained underwear and one glance at the captains body and started to speak,

"Is he…?" but that was as far as he got. Aharon had grabbed him from behind and in one swift movement he held the knife across the throat of the wretch.

"Where is my father?" he demanded.

Again the sailor began to speak but Aharon interrupted him.

"No, you can show us where he is. Lie down on the floor face downwards, "arms out away from your body.

The mariner eagerly complied. If they could kill a powerful man like the captain what chance did he have, he thought?

Aharon searched the man and removed his own knife, which he quickly handed to Miriam. Then while Miriam sat on the almost motionless body of the sailor, knife pressed into the nape of his neck, Aharon cut up bed sheets to make ropes with which to secure their prisoner. Once the man was securely trussed up with his hands behind his back Aharon pulled him to his feet and instructed him to show them the location of their father, Don Jose.

The first mate, Manuel and most of the crew were on deck still busy battling against the ravages of the storm. Of the three crewmembers below deck, one was their captive and the other two were in the deep sleep that is only enjoyed by the totally exhausted and the totally intoxicated. There was no guard on José's cell. A stout door and a strong lock were considered more than adequate.

Their new prisoner had a bunch of keys hanging from his belt and the correct one was quickly located. The room was pitch black and the stench made them all retch. Then in a corner lying on the hard wooden floor they saw their father. He was of course filthy and unshaven and at first he did not even look up to see who had entered.

"Dad," Aharon cried, "Are you all right?"

Jose at first thought he was dreaming. This was just an apparition of his son and daughter. He had by now reconciled himself to dying of disease and starvation in the filthy lock-up.

When they located Rebecca in the galley, she almost fainted. She knew that her husband had been in the lockup but in her wildest nightmares she could not have imagined the state he was now in. As for her daughter, charging around the ship in bloodstained underwear: this was completely beyond her comprehension.

Rebecca rushed up to her husband and daughter and tried to embrace them both at the same time.

"Are you hurt?" she asked her daughter. "Where did all that blood come from?"

"Mum, I am fine," Miriam assured her, "But Dad is very weak. Please let him sit down."

"What has happened?" Rebecca again enquired. "Why are you undressed?"

"Look Mum, I will tell you all about it later but first we have work to do."

A certain amount of information was essential not only for the passengers gathered in the Galley but also for Jose who was equally horrified by his daughter's appearance. He was feeling better by the minute and was gratefully chewing a large crust of stale bread as if it was a banquet. He sipped a mug of water as he listened to a brief description of recent events and they discussed what now needed to be done. Even without the full details of how Captain Alfonso had received his just deserts both Jose and Rebecca realised that their difficult, argumentative daughter whose stubborn and often arrogant ways had caused them much grief, was a heroine and the saviour of them all.

First they must neutralise the crewmembers below deck. The four passengers easily overpowered the two sleeping members of the crew who found themselves keeping their shipmate company in the lockup before they were hardly awake enough to recognise their predicament. The main problem now was to contact the first mate Manuel, on the bridge, to ascertain where his sympathies lay. They knew he was one of the conversos, a Jew who had accepted the cross and he had been more than friendly and helpful when they had come on board. The other five crewmen were an unknown quantity.

At first they thought of trying to entice them below, one at a time, overpowering them and locking them up with their mates in the cell. The storm had died down considerably at that time but none of the passengers had the slightest idea how to sail a large sea-going vessel even in calm weather. Finally Jose suggested that young Elazar should be sent up to the bridge with a message apparently from the captain to Manuel, to come below for new instructions. Manuel accepted the summons at face value and passed the wheel to another sailor. As soon as he descended the steps Aharon and Yitzchak grabbed him and with a knife held at his throat he was taken to Miriam's cabin.

Manuel took in the situation very quickly and despite having his arms pinioned behind him and a knife at the ready he began first to smile, then to chuckle and finally to laugh.

"What is so funny?" Jose demanded.

Manuel gestured towards the corpse now lying on the floor.

"That man was the most evil tyrant ever to sail out of Cadiz," he said.

"Not only me, but all the crew will be delighted to be free of him. He had only two friends on board, Ramon and Fernandez-they were sleeping below decks, where are they now?" he enquired anxiously.

Manuel, no longer laughing, glanced nervously towards the door as if expecting the two acolytes to suddenly appear.

"Don't worry," Jose assured him, "We have three men securely locked up in the cell. And that includes your two friends," he added.

"Aharon, I think you can remove the knife now," Jose continued, "Manuel, can you sail the ship without the captain and his friends?

"Normally the answer would be yes but we have been blown miles westwards by the storm and our sailing instruments have been smashed to pieces by the waves. I hope to be able to get us back on course by using the sun, moon and stars to plot our location but when I tried to plot our position just an hour ago we seemed to be far to the north west of where we should be now."

"One thing is for sure, the captain may have been a good seaman and navigator in his own way but Ramon and Hernandez were good for nothing ruffians. The only use they were to Alfonso was to gamble and booze with him below deck and to go out whoring with him when we put into port," he continued.

"So does this mean that the other five on deck are trustworthy?" Jose enquired.

"Yes," Manuel responded, "they are all my friends and two of them, Jaime and Pedro, are conversos the same as me."

"Manuel," Jose answered, "If you have any weapons about your person we are going to take them from you. I am inclined to accept your sincerity but I have too much at stake to take any chances with the lives of my family and friends."

Turning to Aharon and Yitzchak, Jose instructed,

"Search him thoroughly and then release him. Our first task then will be to release our third prisoner once Manuel has identified the scoundrels Ramon and Hernandez."

It turned out that the third prisoner was Cristobal, the sailor who had loaned his knife to Miriam the previous day. He was more than grateful to be set free not just from the revolting lockup but also from the company of Ramon and Hernandez who were already threatening him with injury and death if he tried to stop them satisfying their unnatural lust upon his person.

Cristobal told them that, contrary to what she thought, he had seen through Miriam's little subterfuge with the knife. He guessed what she had in mind to do to the captain but doubted her ability to achieve the desired result. He told them that the captain had boasted to most of the crew of what he was going to do to the *little Jewish Whore* ever since Jose and his party had come aboard. Only Ramon and

Hernandez were impressed. The others, including himself, Cristobal and Manuel were horrified and terrified of the consequences of a mutiny. They sought in vain for alternative ways to save the Spanish gentleman, Don Jose and his family.

Jose, Aharon, Yitzchak and young Elazar escorted Manuel and Cristobal on to the deck where Manuel called all the crew together and recounted to them everything that had transpired below deck. Jose then told them that Manuel was now appointed captain and it was the duty of them all to work with him to bring the vessel back on course.

Predictably, the news of the demise of Captain Alfonso was received enthusiastically. However, Jose still felt it prudent, except for the knives needed for maintaining the ship's rigging and for cutting up food, to take all other potential weaponry under his direct control.

The funeral of the late unlamented Captain was as unceremonious as the scoundrel deserved. His body was wrapped in sailcloth and it took four sailors to drag the huge heavy bundle up the steps to the deck. There, Jose asked Cristobal to intone the usual Christian burial service for those who lost their lives at sea. Then with no eulogy the body slid down a plank into the ocean for the benefit of the sharks.

Sadly, the weather having initially improved began to deteriorate once again. The crew, however, worked cheerfully under Captain Manuel and the passengers volunteered to do all within their power to assist in the smooth running of the ship. Somehow, no matter how violently the ship was assailed by wind and sea all aboard seemed to be cured of their seasickness.

CHAPTER SEVEN

THE PEOPLE WATCHER

NATANYA-ISRAEL 1991

A small group of United Nations soldiers was sitting at one of the tables situated on the pavement outside the Geffen Cafe-Bar. From this vantage point, they could survey the main square in Natanya. The busy tourist area was always floodlit and as a result even in the blackness of the Mediterranean night, the young men could lean back in princely fashion to watch the endless parade of visitors and residents enjoying a promenade in the warm, balmy, evening air of the resort. Their main interest, not surprisingly, was girls. They watched in silence, punctuated only by the occasional low whistle of appreciation, as the wide selection of members of the female sex strolled by. Some of the girls, a small minority it must be said, the more provocatively dressed ones, were undoubtedly doing their best to be noticed by the group. There were always a few professional camp followers looking for a good time with the foreign soldiers.

There were five young men at the table. Four of the soldiers were Irish and the fifth, Norwegian. Lars Petersen, a tall strong Viking was the oldest. He was twenty-five and a Corporal. The Irish boys were all between nineteen and twenty-two and had arrived in Israel only two weeks previously. They all knew exactly why they were there. Their job was to act as a buffer between Hizb'ulla and the Palestinian militias on the one side and the Israeli backed South Lebanese Army.

Their true mandate was far from clear, even to their officers and their position was particularly dangerous as none of the opposing forces had much time or respect for them. However, although the young Irish boys had not yet been exposed to active duty, they had learned all about the dangers and quickly convinced themselves that leave time spent in Israel would more than compensate. Sunshine, booze and girls were a heady mixture for young men thousands of miles from home.

The four Irish soldiers were Sean, Eamonn, Joseph and Michael and apart from ogling the girls their main occupation that evening was downing half-litres of Maccabi or Goldstar beer. There was no doubt that Joseph had travelled much further than his compatriots to arrive at this table in Natanya. The other three were all Dublin boys and were more than familiar with the temptations of modern, city life. Just a year ago Joseph had still been a shepherd boy sitting on a lonely barren hillside and now here he was, apparently fulfilling all the worst fears of his parents. He may have been wearing the uniform of the world's peacekeeping force but to his father he would have seemed totally corrupted by his new friends and environment. McGillicuddys Reeks and all they stood for seemed to be light years away from Private Joseph Allbarrow.

Joseph had been trained and drilled by tough sergeants and instructors. They had sworn at him and screamed at him and subjected him to almost intolerable physical punishment. These men were totally different to the pleasant, paternalistic recruiting sergeants he had previously encountered. He had imagined that the latter were typical of the army: now he knew otherwise. However, he had emerged from the tough course, as a smart strong alert young soldier ready to face whatever his country required of him. Eventually he had been posted to the border with Northern Ireland. It was the job of his platoon to patrol bandit country, as it was called. They were there to stop IRA terrorists infiltrating the northern neighbour to commit their acts of violence. He had acquitted himself well and had then been offered a posting to UNIFIL. This meant he would again be working in bandit country and apparently dealing with even more violence than that he had seen in Ireland. However, his spare time could be spent in the Holy Land and despite his parents worst fears to the contrary, he was still a God fearing member of the Allbarrow clan.

Visiting the Holy Land had always been his dream. At school, be the subject History, Geography or Bible all he ever wanted to hear of was the little land where Abraham, Isaac and Jacob, David and Solomon, Mary and Jesus had lived. Joseph jumped at the chance and after further training he was flown out to Ben Gurion Airport in Israel with a number of other recruits. He was amazed by the sights that greeted him at the airport, the crowds of people, the aircraft on the tarmac from so many different parts of the world and the signs in Hebrew, English, Russian and Arabic. Joseph, to the best of his knowledge, had never seen Hebrew writing before but for some curious reason, it looked vaguely familiar. He puzzled over this as he walked through the airport and finally decided that he must have seen the script on television newscasts during his year in barracks in Ireland.

Traffic jams had been a shocking spectacle for him when he first arrived in Dublin. Little by little he had learned that this was one of prices one had to pay for living in a crowded city. Israel, on the other hand, he had expected to be a land of lush rolling fields; a land where shepherds in long white robes husbanded their flocks. . The last thing he had expected to see was a motorway, just beyond the airport, that seemed to be crammed with so much traffic that he suspected the entire population of Israel must be in the vicinity at that time.

The first days in camp were spent listening to lectures on the problems of south Lebanon and the usual essential sessions of drilling and training. He was now a proud Irish member of an international force, UNIFIL, and he was determined to acquit himself accordingly. Once training was completed the boys were allowed a short over night leave in Natanya, before going into what could only be realistically called the battle-zone. After checking into a small hotel that specialised in catering for junior UN personnel the five young men had wandered into the square where Lars, an old Natanya 'hand,' had recommended the Geffen Café-Bar.

Apart from the girls, the main treat was watching the fascinating passing parade of all the people. There was a majority of modern secular Israelis. Their attire was indistinguishable from that worn on a warm summer evening by people anywhere in the western world. There were also modern religious Israelis whose dress differed from their secular brothers only in respect of the small skullcap worn by their men folk and the headscarf that invariably covered the hair of the women. Soon Joseph also noticed that the religious women always wore skirts rather than the jeans or pants favoured by the secular Jews. Then there were the Chasidic Jews. These were fewer in number in Natanya. Their women dressed in the identical manner to their modern religious sisters but the men wore black or navy frock coats and many sported heavy looking Trilby or Homburg hats. The Chasidic men also had beards, some quite long and bushy, and some wore beautifully plaited side curls that hung at the sides of their ears. They looked very distinguished and incredibly hot!

The black Jews were a surprise to Joseph. He quickly discovered that they were recent immigrants from Ethiopia. They were all young and mainly religious, if the skullcaps were any kind of indication. There were just a few Arabs. Occasionally an elderly man, probably a Sheikh, Joseph suspected, usually in European clothes but sporting the traditional and identifying Keffiyeh, headdress, passed by. Lars pointed out how relaxed and unconcerned the few passing Arabs were to be so outnumbered by their apparent enemy and commented that there must be a lesson there, somewhere. Eventually Joseph realised that many of the passers by were not Israelis at all, but tourists visiting the popular resort from England, America, France and many other countries.

This was the evening that Joseph became a qualified people-watcher and he pursued his new hobby with great interest. Sadly the coach to ferry them back to the camp was arriving at eleven thirty and they were obliged, reluctantly, to return to the hotel and collect their belongings. So, sad to leave and full of fear and misapprehension of their dangerous assignment, the four new recruits and their far more experienced Norwegian friend, started their journey to the north.

Chapter Eight

Shipwrecked

1492

The storm still showed no sign of abating and Manuel, despite his seamanship found it impossible to locate their position. These were undoubtedly the worst sailing conditions anyone on board had ever encountered. Early spring storms occurred frequently but the duration and intensity of this storm rendered it out on its own as a manifestation of the power that nature could unleash. Jose remembered the story of Jonah and the Whale and he decided that the storm that had occurred then must have been similar to this one.

Without instruments and with the stars completely obliterated from view by the dense black clouds, Manuel became increasingly worried for the safety of the ship and all its passengers and crew. He had taken to standing on the port side gazing at the sky for hours on end. He prayed for a glimpse, just one glimpse of a recognisable alignment of stars but all he saw was blackness. Then the longed for break in the clouds occurred and he could hardly believe his eyes. They were leagues to the north and west of where they were supposed to be. Manuel turned to dash back to the bridge to do some calculations to try and confirm their position. As he did so the jib, which all his training had told him always to watch out for, swung across and dealt him a hefty blow to the head. The acting captain fell to the ground, unconscious and bleeding from a nasty gash on the forehead.

He was found by a crewman patrolling the deck and carried below but all attempts to revive him failed.

Jose called the other crewmen together and enquired as to their ability to navigate the vessel. One by one they had to admit that they could hold a steady course with the wheel but knew neither where they were heading nor how to find out that essential information.

The morning after Manuel's accident the sun was just visible rising in the east and Jose knew that they were sailing westwards, completely the wrong direction. The vessel turned and miraculously and mercifully the deluge of rain stopped. That was good news but when just half an hour later the wind dropped until they were virtually becalmed, Jose despaired of ever reaching Casablanca.

They all welcomed the peace and quiet. The ship drifted along and after the long period of unremitting noise from the storm all they could hear was the gentle lapping of the almost still sea against the sides of the ship.

"We should thank God we are no longer in any danger," Rebecca said to Jose. She assumed they were on course and if it took longer to arrive at their intended destination she was more than happy, as long as the storm did not return.

No one on board except Jose and Manuel had known how seriously lost they were. Some of the crew were puzzled by the intense cold that they were experiencing on deck but they wrapped up warmly and were happy to see the back of the vicious wind and rain. Now Jose had no one to share his worries. Manuel was still unconscious and his condition was giving serious cause for concern.

"Yes, my dear," he answered his wife, determined to protect her from the knowledge that he knew they must all face eventually. They were totally lost.

And then they saw land. Straight ahead of them were rocks and beyond lay a narrow sandy shore. And behind the shore all they could see, as the ship approached, were huge black looking hills rising ever higher into the distance. There was no sign of a port or of human habitation. Still, it was land and Jose thanked the Lord for delivering them to safety. The helmsman easily found a gap between the rocks and dropped anchor at a safe distance. They had lost one boat in the storm but the other was there on the starboard side and the crew quickly lowered it into the gentle lapping sea. With the exception of the old Rabbi's widow who undertook to sit besides Manuel in case he regained consciousness and two crewmembers left on board, to guard the ship and prisoners, all the passengers and crew went ashore.

The relief of being safely returned to dry land, after the perilous voyage, was certainly sweet. They walked up and down the narrow sandy beach and peered up at the high cliffs towering over them. It was cold and despite being well wrapped up Rebecca began to shiver.

"Where on earth are we?" She asked her husband. "I have never felt cold and damp like this before. I thought Casablanca was at least as hot as Spain. We must be a long way from there."

"My love," Jose admitted, "I have known we were far off course for some time now. However, I have no idea of where we might be."

Suddenly realising that he owed her a better explanation he told her of the loss of the ship's instruments and the lack of navigating ability of the remaining crew. Then he continued,

"I think we might be in Brittany or even England. I imagine they would look like this and be similarly cold."

"Oh, I do hope this is England," Rebecca replied, "If we are near Rochester we can go to my cousin, Pedro Lopez. He is of course a Christian convert but I know he would always help his family when they are in trouble."

"Look, Rebecca," Jose responded. "Please understand that I do not know where we are. To say this place might be England or Brittany is only a guess. We must somehow make our way up those cliffs and then hopefully we will know for certain where we are."

Jose called Aharon and Cristobal to join him as they set out to find a path up the rock face. Fortunately God smiled upon their efforts and they quickly found a spot where the cliffs were a little lower and a crack in the rock had made a natural path that they climbed easily. However the scene that met them filled them with dismay. As far as the eye could see the landscape consisted of dark desolate hills. The only vegetation was tough grass and a few stunted trees that grew in the hollows. The higher reaches of the hills were covered in black boulders and a hazy mist hung over the horizon to the west. There was no evidence of human habitation and the three men returned to the shore deeply depressed.

As they stepped down on to the sand they were met by Yitzchak and young Elazar who excitedly told Jose of a large cave they had discovered, half way up the cliff, in the opposite direction from that taken by Jose, Aharon and Cristobal. The cave proved to be dry and easily accessible even for the women in their long frocks. It could only be two hours until nightfall and three of the sailors were sent off to the ship to bring all the provisions and as many other possessions ashore as the small craft would hold. Jose went with them to bring the Sepher Torah ashore. He was not about to leave it on board when the old Rabbi Yair had lost his life to save it.

It was also decided that with the exception of Manuel who could not leave the vessel and the Rabbi's widow, who would not leave the vessel, all other personnel were to come ashore. This of course included the two prisoners who were secured in irons in case they should attempt an escape, once they were back on dry land. The main cave was an ideal haven. Twenty yards inside it was warm and cosy and large enough to give reasonable privacy to the different groups of travellers. Moreover there was another smaller cave, just a short distance along the same ledge and the two prisoners were to be secured there and guarded throughout the night by members of the crew.

A fire was prepared at the mouth of the larger cave from a variety of driftwood, seaweed and dried grass. It was rather smoky but the gentle sea breeze of the evening ensured that this was no problem. They boiled up water in a huge iron pan brought from the ship and prepared the first square meal any of them had enjoyed since leaving Cadiz.

By nine o'clock all were sound asleep with the sole exception of Cristobal who had volunteered to guard the two prisoners in the other cave.

It was so quiet and peaceful in the large cave that they were all blissfully unaware that the stormy weather had returned while they slept. They were also blissfully unaware that the two scoundrels had tried to overpower Cristobal and that in the ensuing struggle all three had fallen to their deaths from the edge of the cliff.

Jose awoke at five thirty and seeing the first glimmers of dawn had prepared to say his morning prayers. He approached the edge of the cave and was horrified to see that the San Fernando had been hurled by the storm against giant rocks where it had been seriously holed. Only the masts were now visible above the surface. Jose knew without a shadow of doubt, that neither the Rabbi's widow nor Manuel could have had any chance of survival. Nevertheless he sent out the boat to check if either of them had by some miracle, survived. At the same time the sailors were instructed to salvage everything they could from the wreck. Sadly, this proved to be impossible and they returned to recount that the deck had collapsed into the hull thus rendering the recovery of the bodies and the group's possessions, out of the question.

The entire party, Jews and Christians stood on the shore as Jose recited appropriate passages from the Jewish burial services and then together they all intoned in Spanish the twenty-third Psalm. "The Lord is my Shepherd............"

Fortunately the previous evening they had brought ashore all of the ship's remaining provisions and that would be enough for the next three to four weeks. In the meantime it was vital that further sources of food and water be found and plans were set in motion to climb up to the top of the cliff, to explore the hinterland.

Suddenly Aharon remembered the prisoners and scrambled quickly up the path that led to their cave. There was of course no sign of them or of Cristobal. Jumping to the obvious conclusion that the three of them had been in cahoots after all, Aharon started to descend by a series of crags that led down from the cave. Leaping down the last few feet on to the wet sand, he saw them. At first he thought it was a huge bundle of clothes washed ashore from the wreck. As he approached he could see the bloodied face of one of the prisoners. The two scoundrels were of course still chained together and Cristobal was gripping the arm of one man while the other miscreant had his arm locked tightly around Cristobal's neck. Aharon felt deep pangs of guilt. He had totally misjudged Cristobal; that was obvious. He dashed down the narrow beach to tell the others what had transpired.

The arrival of the voyagers in their new land had been beset with tragedy. They hoped and prayed that this was not setting the pattern for their future life in this strange, hard and cold land.

Chapter Nine

A Temporary Home

1492

Once again the black storm clouds lifted and although the sky was hardly the brilliant azure blue of their homeland they could see enough of the sun to know that they were on the southern shore of, in all probability, an island. Jose mused that this probably was England but far beyond Rochester and Kent. He had heard that the Dartmoor area of Cornwall looked as bleak as this place appeared to be. So, he conjectured that if this was Cornwall there should be villages along the coast both to the west and to the east.

By mid-morning two parties each of three men had been organised to climb up the cliffs to explore. The other men and women were all given tasks to undertake in the caves to make them more habitable for their second night ashore.

José's party, consisting of Elazar and Jaime set out to the west as soon as they had arrived at the top of the cliff. Jose had not wanted his younger son to go with him into unknown territory but Elazar had pleaded to be allowed to accompany his father and he had relented. After all he has been through already, Jose decided; a little exploring will be quite tame by comparison.

Yitzchak, Aharon and Pedro went eastwards. Jose had not wanted Yitzchak to leave his pregnant wife Sarah. She had miraculously survived the perilous voyage without any apparent detriment to herself or the new life growing within her.

"Yitzchak," Jose had said. "It would be much better if you stayed on shore to organise the storage of our provisions.

That way you could keep an eye on Sarah, as well. Let one of the sailors go with Aharon and Pedro."

"Sarah is fine, thank God," Yitzchak had replied. "She still has over two months to go and it is more important that I find a permanent home for my little family."

Bidding each other farewell the two groups of explorers set out in opposite directions. They all carefully noted the position of the path that would lead them back down to the beach on their return. It had been Yitzchak's idea to tie an old coloured shirt to the large clump of coarse grass that grew alongside the path. They all set out confident that with a little care and careful observation of the terrain, they would have no difficulty in finding the way back to the marker before nightfall.

José's party walked for over an hour, hugging the cliffs and watching the sun that was now slowly swinging away from their left and would soon be facing them. All they saw was a terrible monotonous sameness. There were large hills and small hills all covered in black rocks and sparse clumps of grass. There was no sign of human habitation or even of animal life in the desolate place. Eventually, just when they were thinking of returning they saw an unusually flat area of land alongside the highest hill they had yet discovered.

"That will make an ideal location for a temporary home," Jose announced. "We can take some of the large rocks from the hillside and build a habitation."

Suddenly young Elazar's practical talents became invaluable as he launched into a convincing and detailed description of how to accomplish the task that his father had just blandly announced.

Jose had previously been surprised by his young son's ability to repair and construct almost anything that needed attention. He was a highly intelligent and sensitive man, knowledgeable in the ways of international trade and finance but far less capable when called upon to achieve even simple practical tasks. It was a mystery from where his younger son had inherited the abilities he displayed. However, Jose had learned to have confidence in the judgement of Elazar, despite his tender years.

The sun was now well to the west and Jose knew they must return immediately but the three of them took careful note of the spot and vowed to return the following day so that construction could commence.

Yitzchak Mendoza and his group had travelled a similar distance in the opposite direction until they too had found a suitable spot for the construction of a temporary abode. They too had been disappointed by the lack of evidence of human habitation. Unlike the other group, however, they did see sheep grazing on a hillside not far beyond the site they had selected for a temporary home. Facing eastwards they had not noticed how low the weak sun now was in the sky and decided to catch a couple of spring lambs for a welcome meat meal. Yitzchak assumed that in the absence of shepherds these sheep must be wild and as such would be fair game to capture. None of them had ever chased sheep around a rocky hill before and for that matter none of them had ever chased sheep at all. The combined efforts of one sailor and the two townsmen were no match for the lambs and all they succeeded in doing was to set off a deafening chorus of bleating from the entire flock. Suddenly Yitzchak noticed that it was almost dark and there they were probably the best part of two hours walk from the path down to the beach.

"Come on boys," he called out to his two companions, "It's almost night; we had better forget the lambs and get back or we will never find our way."

By this time Jose and his party were safely back at base and found Rebecca, Miriam and the others waiting anxiously.

They had prepared delicious soup from the dried vegetables among the ship's provisions. Two of the sailors had been out in the boat and using makeshift nets had caught some unfamiliar looking fish. Rebecca had examined these and pronounced them as Kosher having both fins and scales. They were now frying on the fire and smelt absolutely wonderful.

Sarah meanwhile had been resting in the cave and when she heard voices she came out to greet her husband.

"Where is Yitzchak?" She enquired anxiously.

"He was with the other party," Jose replied soothingly, "I'm sure they will be back any minute now. He is with Aharon and Pedro," he added reassuringly.

A further hour passed and still there was no sign of the missing trio.

"We must eat," Rebecca said. "Sarah, please help me to pass round the soup otherwise the fish will be burned to a cinder."

Sarah nodded glumly. She was now desperately worried as to the fate of her husband but they had all worked hard that day and the dinner could not be delayed any longer.

The meal should have been a treat but instead it was swallowed in a worried silence and without the appreciation it deserved.

They had long since finished eating and cleared away when noises were heard of people descending the rocky path. Thank God, it was Yitzchak, Aharon and Pedro and all breathed a sigh of relief.

Jose ran up the beach to meet them.

"What on earth happened to you?" he enquired. Despite the cool night they were pouring with sweat and panting from a long run.

"Let's get to the cave and I will tell you," Yitzchak replied with a note of urgency in his voice.

The entire group now consisting of the five members of the Alvaro family, Sarah Mendoza, her daughter Leah and the five surviving crewmen sat on the sandy ground of the cave to listen to what Yitzchak had to report. Aharon and Pedro of course, could have interrupted and tried to add to the story but they listened to their companion at first with the same rapt silence as the others. Yitzchak began by recounting the uneventful walk to site where he had chosen to build his first home in this new land. He told them about the sheep and lambs they had located and which they had assumed were living in the wild. He explained about their foolhardy attempt to capture two of the animals for their evening meal and then came the biggest surprise of all.

"Suddenly we realised that it was almost dark and that we must immediately retrace our steps to find the path down to the beach," he told them. "When we turned we saw the 'them.' They must have been watching us trying to catch the lambs."

"Who?" Jose enquired, uncharacteristically irritated by the ponderous presentation affected by Yitzchak. "Who was watching you?" he again enquired.

"Three strange, ragged looking men," Yitzchak at last explained.

"So, did you speak to them?" Jose asked.

"No," Yitzchak responded. "We called to them but they ran off. I think they followed us all the way back to the path, though," he continued.

"We had feeling they were watching us from behind the lower hills and mounds as we walked."

A buzz of excitement had run through the group during this exchange. So this island is inhabited after all, they thought.

"You say they were strange and ragged looking," Jose questioned. "Can you add to that description?"

"Yes," came a voice from the audience. It was Pedro who had probably seen far more outlandish and primitive people on his travels than Yitzchak or any of José's party had ever encountered. Pedro stood up. He was a small dark-haired man of some thirty years. Somehow or other, whatever conditions he had to endure, he always managed to look neat and well groomed. He had come through a voyage on storm-tossed seas culminating in a shipwreck. He had slept in a cave and trudged all day through damp muddy terrain and still his hair was sleeked down and his sailor's uniform remained smart and presentable.

"I have seen men like that in Brittany, in the northern lands and in Scotland," he told his companions.

"These three men were tall and strong with blond beards and although to a Spanish gentleman like Yitzchak their clothing looked ragged, it looked to me more like woollen, home-spun and is no doubt warm and probably quite well made."

"These people will not be savages and indeed they are probably Christians. They are, however, simple country folk and will be very wary of people like us," he concluded.

"Thank you, Pedro," Jose answered, "That was a very useful contribution. So do you think we may be in Brittany or Scotland possibly?"

"No, Don Jose," Pedro responded. "From the look of the three men either of those two locations would be possible but the terrain here is more like Dartmoor in England or possibly even Ireland."

They all gasped. They had never even considered Ireland but to those schooled in Geography that idea began to present itself as a distinct possibility.

Despite the news Jose knew they must all try to sleep. Tomorrow they would try again to contact the inhabitants of this place and even more importantly, they must start to construct temporary abodes in the areas they had selected. Jose climbed under the sheets alongside Rebecca. He lay there agonising about their future but the comfort of sleep refused to still his tortured brain. He turned over and realised that Rebecca was also awake. She was gazing at him with an expression that seemed to show fear, sadness and pity in equal measure.

"My poor Jose," she whispered. "What a burden you now have to carry. In Cordoba taking care of us all was easy. You had the money and the power and you lived in a world, your world, a world you totally understood."

"Suddenly, through no fault of your own, we are plunged into this strange hard place," she continued. "What will become of you and what will become of us all?" she ventured, a little sob creeping into her voice.

Jose put out his arm and Rebecca rested her head on it as she nestled closer to him, desperate for the comfort and re-assurance she knew he could not provide.

"We must hope and pray for deliverance. Surely a ship will pass by soon. I will ask the sailors to light fires on the beach each night to show our position."

Jose did not really believe this as his logical mind had long since calculated that there could be no reason on earth for ships to venture anywhere near this desolate place.

"Come on darling," he continued. "We must get some sleep. We have huge tasks ahead of us tomorrow. "

Still wide-awake he lay there conjecturing .His mind was in turmoil over the many problems he knew they must face. The huge drums of fresh water they had floated from the ship to the beach, would only last another two or three weeks. The stock of provisions may last another two months. They had to find food and water quickly. Otherwise they would all perish from thirst and starvation.

Why oh why, had he gone to Cadiz? He agonised. But then he had no choice and if God wished to test him he must find answers to all these difficulties. *At least we have shelter in this cave.* Jose tried to rationalise. . And tomorrow we will start to construct better accommodation.

Rebecca was now sound asleep and he turned to study her beautiful face. How could such an elegant Spanish lady who had been accustomed to having servants to obey her every whim, survive this virtual hell? Then he remembered how she had been forced to scrub the decks on the ship. He shuddered as he thought of what might have been if not for his usually wayward daughter. Both Rebecca & Miriam are made of sterner stuff than I ever appreciated, he thought. With God's help we will adjust and build a new life for ourselves.

The next few days were indeed spent in building a stone house for the Alvaro family. Then they constructed a smaller but similar construction for Yitzchak and Sarah Mendoza and their growing family. All the men worked as a team first on one project and then on the other under the direction of Elazar the youngest member of the group. Each night they returned to the caves where Rebecca and Miriam had devised a series of tasty fish meals that were enthusiastically devoured by the hungry men.

Rebecca silently wondered at the radical change in Miriam. In Cordoba, if she had even suggested that Miriam should tidy her room she would have been met with tantrums. Here she could not have asked for a more considerate and helpful daughter. Miriam had come through an ordeal totally beyond the scope of her mother's worst nightmares and seemed, incredibly, to have had her character transformed and strengthened by the experience. She had left Spain as a spoilt child and had metamorphosed into a strong, beautiful and resolute young woman.

During the building period there were no more sightings of the native inhabitants of the place. They decided that if Pedro's assessment had been correct they were keeping away from the new arrivals and probably spied on their building progress from hidden vantage points in the hills.

They had discussed building a further stone house where the five sailors, Pedro, Jaime, Domingo, Julio and Bernardo could live but the lure of the sea was still strong and the five men had decided to remain in the cave for the time being and make it more habitable.

"We can live on fish," Julio had suggested. "In fact if we catch fish for you," he continued, "maybe we can trade it with you for lamb. Also I am sure you will be able to find edible vegetables once you do some more exploring."

"Our first priority must be to find fresh water," Jose quietly reminded Julio.

The next day Jose, Aharon and Julio set out to find fresh water. The other men remained behind to assist in the final construction of the stone houses. This proved to be an easy task. The higher reaches of the hills had numerous mountain streams within easy reach of the new habitations. This was one blessing of the damp, rainy and often misty climate. Probably the only one, Jose decided, but then he must thank God for any gift that would alleviate their plight.

The next day when they all assembled after morning prayers Jose turned his attention to their food needs.

"I hope we will be able to catch some lambs after Yitzchak's first attempt was such a disaster. As for vegetables the only thing I have seen is coarse grass," Jose announced. "However," he continued thoughtfully, "The men that Yitzchak's party saw that day must live on something other than meat and fish. Maybe we will be able to trade after all and not only with each other."

So, just four weeks after their enforced arrival in this inhospitable looking land, the two families moved the pitifully small residue of their belongings to survive the shipwreck, into their new and considered temporary abodes.

Chapter Ten

Dalia

Jerusalem 1992

Private Joseph Allbarrow sat alone sipping an ice-cold Goldstar beer outside the Geffen Café-Bar in Natanya. He always came back to the Geffen when he was on leave and his mind always went back to his first visit there over a year ago. Two of the Irish boys who had been his companions that night had now returned to Ireland. The remaining one was on duty just north of the Israeli/Lebanese border. It was Lars, or rather the memory of Lars that always drew him back here. Lars had been his friend and mentor and he had been standing at the checkpoint next to him when the car had pulled up. Lars had said to leave it to him and leaned forward to ask the driver for his identification. It had all happened so quickly and so horribly silently. One moment his friend was bending down to look into the old Mercedes and the next moment he was lying on the ground in a fast spreading pool of his own blood. It had taken precious seconds for Joseph to realise what had happened and in that time the driver had engaged gear and shot off into the area policed by the Hizb'ulla Militia. Joseph had let off a stream of bullets in the car's wake but he knew this was an empty gesture. Dashing to where his friend lay he saw the knife embedded almost to the hilt in Lars' chest and he knew that the kindly Norwegian had breathed his last. There had been an enquiry into the incident but those responsible were never apprehended. This was eight months ago now but Joseph's eyes still filled with tears when he re-lived the incident.

He picked up the letter with its Irish stamp and began to re-read it. Nothing much changed on McGillicuddys Reeks.

His father and mother were well, the letter reported. His brothers and sisters were all growing up and were achieving good results at the village school. Alan was working well with his father and they were looking forward to a good sale of young lambs at the market.

Once the enquiry over the tragic death of Lars was completed Joseph had been offered a long leave back home in Ireland but he had declined. He was not yet ready to face his family. He knew he must have become like a stranger in their eyes and they would be the same in his. Sure, he still loved them but their lives were so different now: literally worlds apart. He preferred to remain in Israel and to explore the country whenever a leave came up.

In the camp Joseph mixed well with the other men but since the death of Lars he valued his own company and often took trips where his fellow travellers were tourists rather than soldiers. Joseph wore civilian clothes on these occasions and within the bounds of common civility he discouraged too much socialising with the other members of the tour. In this lone fashion he had visited Bethlehem and Nazareth and had to admit to himself deep disappointment with each of these trips. It was not that the places were uninteresting. After all they were associated with Jesus and Mary. The problem was he, himself. He departed feeling no more spiritually uplifted than when he had arrived. He could not understand this as all his life he had longed to see these towns with their holy history. Why did the manger where Jesus was born not thrill him, as expected?

This night in Natanya Joseph was still in his UN uniform but tomorrow he would set off in jeans and jumper for the holy city of Jerusalem. Tomorrow he would see the Stations of the Cross, the Garden of Gethsemane, the Church of the

Holy Sepulchre and all the other places where Jesus had walked, talked and preached.

In the morning he rose early. He loved the Israeli breakfast. He found the cheeses particularly to his liking and had now developed a taste for the tasty herrings that gave him a thirst enough to down three large mugs of hot, strong coffee. He often thought how different this breakfast was from the fried eggs and occasional rasher of bacon he had consumed at home.

The tour bus left the main square at eight o'clock in the morning and after battling its way up Herzl Street it passed the huge shopping mall and turned right onto the main highway that connected the cities of Tel Aviv and Haifa. As usual Joseph had purchased a guidebook and he settled back to study and absorb all the information he could devour about his final destination. After driving along the Ayalon, the eight-lane motorway that connected north Tel Aviv to the south side of the city the tour bus took the left fork and they were on the road to Jerusalem. All this area was familiar to Joseph, at least as far as Ben Gurion Airport. He could hardly believe that it was only a year ago that he had arrived as a raw recruit. There was something about Israel that made him feel that he belonged. He still loved Ireland but what was it that tied him so firmly to this hot, dusty and often violent country? Beyond the airport, the road started to climb upwards into the hills. The sight of the wonderful scenery spellbound all aboard, including Joseph. It seemed like only a few minutes earlier they had been on the edge of a huge sprawling city and what open spaces there were seemed flat and uninteresting. Now every bend in the road showed the passengers a new panorama of trees, mountains and valleys. In these valleys Joseph could see buildings of great antiquity alternating with modern settlements in gleaming white stucco.

The bus was not full and Joseph had taken a window seat. He had placed his holdall on the adjoining seat as he hoped this would discourage anyone from taking the outer position. Years of sitting on hard black rocks on barren hillsides watching his sheep had made him into a loner and in the incommunicative family, in which he had been raised, he was unaware of the pleasures of sharing experiences with others. It was perfectly true that he had become quite close with Lars but then Lars was almost like a father figure for the young Joseph. Of course he chatted to the other soldiers in his platoon but always he erected a barrier beyond which no one was allowed to go. He remained a private person and was accepted as such by his mates.

Then he saw the old tanks at the side of the road. They had been made into memorials for the heroes of the War of Independence who had perished there trying to break the siege of Jerusalem in 1948. He turned round to stare at the sight and was startled from his own thoughts by a female voice behind him, which was obviously addressing him.

The voice belonged to a breathtakingly beautiful young, dark-haired woman in her early twenties. She had spoken to him in English with the almost unerring ability of Israelis to assess the nationality of anyone they wished to address.

"Can you imagine what it must have been like to ride in one of those death traps?"

"No, err no!" Joseph managed to stammer. He was shy of girls. Certainly he was only too happy to sit outside the Geffen watching the passing parade. Although he was a religiously raised young man he was still a man and he had his little fantasies. However both in Dublin and in Natanya when the other boys started to buy drinks and chat to the sort of girls who frequented bars Joseph became tongue-tied and usually excused himself from the party. Sometimes girls approached him when he was having a quiet drink. He was a good-looking young man with straight black hair and intense smouldering dark eyes. In uniform he looked particularly handsome and distinguished. He had never decided if it was the in-built discretion that resulted from his upbringing or just natural shyness but just within the bounds of courtesy he quickly discouraged all female comers.

At night, in bed and alone with his thoughts he had often challenged himself to respond to the next female to approach him and to lose his virginity. In the cold light of day he was either too scared or too proper to take this course.

Having answered the girl in the seat behind him, Joseph treated her to a polite little smile and turned round to face the front of the bus. He decided to pick up the guidebook again and began to read. However, once again he heard the voice from behind,

"Is it your first visit to Jerusalem?" the soft musical voice enquired.

Joseph swivelled round in the double seat, his back to the window and mustering the same sad courteous little smile as before he answered,

"Yes, indeed it is."

"You're Irish," the girl responded with a twinkle in her eye. "I have friends in Jerusalem who come from Dublin. Where are you from?"

"Who, me," Joseph stammered, "I'm from the south. You'll never have heard of McGillicuddys Reeks, I am sure."

He made to turn back but the young lady persisted.

"My name is Dalia Mendoza, what's yours?"

"Joseph Allbarrow, Private Joseph Allbarrow of the Irish army," he told her and was then amazed to hear himself telling her that he was on secondment to UNIFIL.

"So you're not Jewish," she enquired surprised to learn his identity and profession.

"No," he replied with a little laugh, "I'm Catholic. I never did hear of a single Jew in McGillicuddys Reeks. Dublin to be sure, but in the Reeks never, that's for certain."

He had never encountered a girl like this Dalia. She was without doubt what they called a 'respectable' girl, he decided. From where he was sitting he could only see the top half of her body. She was wearing a crisp white cotton blouse buttoned up to the neck and a Denim jacket. She wore no make-up except a little lipstick and eyeliner and her straight black hair was scooped back. She wore discreet pearl earrings and everything he could see appeared tasteful and understated. Joseph had not realised that he was staring at her and that he had absorbed all this detail until she said,

"Well, have I passed the examination?"

Joseph coloured and stuttered an apology to which she replied,

"It's OK; I took the opportunity to study you during the military inspection. Are you sure you are not a Sergeant? That's what they do; check you are properly turned out, don't they?"

Joseph was fascinated to listen to the girl's speech and accent. Her English was faultless and the only trace of it not being her first language was the slightly guttural 'R' sounds.

He was amazed to hear himself continuing the conversation.

"Where do you come from?" he enquired.

"Me," she replied in surprise, "I'm from here, Israel. I'm a tour guide. At least during the university vacation," she continued.

"Are you our guide for today?" he asked her.

"No," she explained, "but I work for this company and I was just getting a lift back home to Jerusalem."

She is so easy to talk to, Joseph mused, and so beautiful.

"I wish you were our tour guide today," Joseph heard himself say.

What a gentle sincere young man, Dalia mused and so different to the usual run of foreign soldiers.

"I only decided to go home first thing this morning," Dalia explained. "I had a day off and I miss Jerusalem so much, when I am away. I thought I would spend the day in town and then surprise the family when they come home from work."

"I would be delighted to be your personal tour guide for today, if you like."

Joseph was secretly delighted and accepted the offer with alacrity.

Dalia, however, was having second thoughts. This young man worries me, she pondered. He is so easy to talk to and so handsome. He is just the type of man I always dreamed of meeting but he is not Jewish. If I spend any amount of time with him we are going to build a relationship. And that can lead to only one outcome-heartbreak.

"Look, Joseph," Dalia said after a short lapse in the conversation. "I am going to have to let you down. I just remembered that I have some work for the University that must be handed in tomorrow. I know I offered to show you round but I had clean forgotten my other commitment."

Joseph looked so crestfallen that Dalia was tempted to change her mind again. However, she was determined not to get into a situation that would hurt her family, her friends, this fine young man and herself.

"Don't worry," Joseph managed to say, "I will still enjoy the tour with the official guide-but not as much as if you had been able to accompany me. I do understand. Maybe another time," he finished lamely.

After that, conversation ceased and Joseph turned round to watch the scenery as the tour bus crept up the final hills and into the Holy City. He knew he was going to enjoy this trip but how much more he would have enjoyed it had Dalia been his guide.

The first stop was the Jaffa Gate to the Old City and when they disembarked Dalia shook his hand solemnly and set off for her home. As she walked away, she turned and called to him in Hebrew, *'Lehitraot.'* He knew that this meant something like the English "See you soon," and for some reason that one Hebrew word made him feel much happier and he set out with the rest of the group into the Old City ready to enjoy all the ancient historical sites and buildings.

Chapter Eleven

Friends or Foes

Ireland 1492

The Alvaro family spent the first few days in their new home organising themselves and carefully creating storage areas for their belongings. There was no timber available so Elazar used small rocks and stones to create divisions between rooms and even built something approximating to cupboards for their clothing. In addition a special area was created where the Sepher Torah could be maintained in dignity and safety.

Food was now becoming a problem as, other than the fish that the crewmen fetched every two or three days, the provisions from the ship, particularly flour and dried vegetables were disappearing at a frighteningly fast rate. Jose realised that it was vital to find the local inhabitants, to befriend them and to offer to trade with them. All he had to barter with, except for one Gold bar, were some of their own personal belongings. It remained to be seen if these articles would be of interest to the peasants described by Pedro.

He had no means of contacting his cousins in Italy, North Africa and the Turkish Empire who were the custodians of nearly all his wealth. He desperately needed to get in touch with them. To do so, however, he needed to know for certain the name of this rugged inhospitable land. Then, he needed to find a port with ships that would either take them all from this God-forsaken place or at least carry messages to his relatives who would arrange their rescue.

Jose decided to take Aharon with him in his search for inhabitants. They spent the Sabbath day as usual in prayer and relaxation and the following morning, Sunday, they set of to explore what lay to the west. They walked or climbed up and down the bleakest of bleak Black Hills across rubble strewn valleys through rain and thick swirling mist but not a sign of life, human or otherwise, did they encounter. They returned home at sunset deeply disappointed but determined the following day to skirt the huge mountain that lay immediately behind them and to explore to the north. It took over two hours to skirt the mountain and the vista before them seemed to offer only more of the same. However they walked on and just half an hour later they saw sheep grazing on the lower reaches of a hillside.

Jose was not about to make the mistake Yitzchak had made and waste their time trying to catch one of the animals. So father and son walked on together until a sudden noise behind them made them stop and turn to ascertain what had occurred. However there was nothing to be seen and they made to continue walking when a rock, obviously thrown from the adjoining hillside came flying towards them.

That could only have been man's work, Jose decided.

"Come on, Aharon," he said. "There has to be someone up there but they don't seem to be very friendly."

As the pair walked determinedly towards a small hillock, a further rain of small stones fell just short of their path.

"That seems to be the place from which the missiles are emanating," Aharon said. As they approached, however, the missiles all but tailed off and Jose commented,

"They seem to be throwing these more as a token discouragement than to actually hit us."

About one hundred metres from the hillock the pair stopped and Jose started to call out greetings in a variety of languages. First he tried Castilian, and then Arabic followed by Hebrew and finally Latin. The sound echoed eerily in the surrounding hills. Then Jose and Aharon heard the bleating of large numbers of sheep obviously disturbed from their grazing by the reverberations of José's voice. It was impossible to identify the direction from which the bleating originated, as at its crescendo, it seemed to be coming at them from all sides. Gradually the noise died away and peace returned.

"Whoever these people are," Jose said sadly, "can't they see we are just two men and that we pose no threat to them?"

The words were hardly out of his mouth when Aharon exclaimed,

"Look Dad, on the left side of the hill."

There were three; no four and finally they saw six men. They were all tall with long blond hair and beards. Their clothing looked bulky and untidy, just as Yitzchak and Pedro had led them to expect. Slowly they walked forward until only some thirty metres separated them and then they stopped, gazing at the two newcomers with a mixture of curiosity, belligerency and apprehension.

Jose raised his two arms over his head and called.

"Pax, Salaam, Shalom, we come in peace."

It was probably no more than one minute but it seemed like an eternity during which the men just stood and stared. Then nodding to each other they began to move slowly and warily forward.

The contrast in appearance between the two groups was very marked. The two Spanish Jews were tall and slim with dark hair and short pointed beards. Even though it was travel stained and worn, their clothing still looked elegant, colourful and expensive. The six local men, however, all wore uniform dark grey thick woollen tweeds and two of them wore crude jackets made from sheepskin.

The distance between the two groups was now no more than ten metres and again the locals stopped. Jose slowly unbuttoned his sword belt and handed it to his son. Then with his arms before him and his hands open he took a few tentative steps forward. The men whispered to one another and one of them slowly pulled a long, evil looking knife from a scabbard at his side and handed it to his neighbour. He also carried a large wooden club and that too he handed over. Now he stepped forward and within a few steps the two men were facing each other. Jose held out his two hands again to show he came in friendship and the blond local did likewise.

Jose had a good knowledge of four languages but the words that now emanated from the other man were totally unrecognisable. Jose could speak neither French nor English but he had heard these tongues often enough to know it was neither. Jose shook his head and smiled. He bowed a courtly bow but this brought no response. Then he gestured with his hands for the uncouth looking man to take his two hands in his and they stood motionless like this for a few moments. This obviously had the desired effect as the other five men now came forward smiling and nodding. Jose called for Aharon to join them and all seven stood in a circle.

"Jose," he said pointing to himself. "Jose," the men responded nodding and smiling.

Then Jose pointed to his son. "Aharon," he said. That proved to be a bit more difficult for the men to pronounce but they all tried.

Then Jose pointed to the leader of the group.

"Patrick," he said in a strange thick accent.

"Ah, Patrique," Jose repeated. He had heard this name before or at least other versions of it. He recognised it as the name of a Christian Saint and this confirmed what Pedro had said about the people probably being Christians. And if they were Christians Jose mused, they must know Latin.

"Pax," he repeated again. This time there was a response.

"Pax," Patrick replied.

"Missa," the Latin word for Mass he intoned solemnly, "Padre, Filio et Spiritus Sanctus," he continued.

It quickly transpired that the only Latin the group knew was what they heard regularly in Church. To use it as a language of everyday communication was quite beyond them.

Jose often used Latin, as it was one of the main languages of international commerce at the time. But to these people it was a barely understood Holy Language. As such, it was often repeated by the congregation, parrot fashion, without any real knowledge of what the words meant. They were praying and as long as the Holy Trinity understood that was all that mattered.

The group continued to smile at each other and even to pat each other on the shoulder but as to verbal communication, it was impossible. Jose realised they must learn the local language if they were to trade with these people and to discover from them where and how they lived. At least today they had made a start. They no longer saw each other as enemies.

Jose bowed and nudged Aharon to do likewise and they pointed to the sun, now quickly descending in the western sky. The others understood and turned to leave, waving their arms in farewell. Their leader, Patrick muttered something that sounded like *Sloncher* and the Spaniards started their long walk back to the new stone house. Glancing over his shoulder, in the gathering dusk, Jose could just make out their new friends climbing the hills and rounding up herds of sheep. So that is one question answered, he thought, they are shepherds.

Chapter Twelve

Rabbi Yossi

Jerusalem 1992

Joseph loved Jerusalem. The heady mixture of the very old and the very new was fascinating. After the official tour he decided to return to the Old City. He had seen all or most of the Christian sites. They were certainly very interesting but he could not help questioning to himself how genuine some of them were? The Stations of the Cross were particularly difficult to accept. He knew from school that Queen Helena, mother of the first Christian Roman Emperor Constantine had discovered them. He could not help but conjecture on what basis she had been able to identify each spot, when Jerusalem had been raised to the ground by the heathen Romans, after the time of Jesus and long before her visit. However, the priests in the village school had always taught him to have faith and as a good Catholic boy he must put such thoughts out of his mind.

Joseph had also climbed the narrow path to the twin Mosques of Omar & Al Aksa. The tour guide had explained that this hill was the site of the Jewish Temples. He also told them that it was from here that according to their tradition, the Muslim Prophet Mohamed had flown up to heaven on a winged and fiery steed.

Joseph wondered to himself what had made him wish to return to the Old City after the tour. He had seen everything of interest to all three religions. However, his footsteps were inexorably leading him back through the narrow crowded passageways to what he had always called the Wailing Wall. The tour Guide had explained that the correct name was the Western Wall and this was the holiest site, in all of Israel, for Jews. It was the one remaining wall of the Temple and looking down the excavation shafts he could see evidence of even more ancient construction on the site.

"The first Temple was built here by King Solomon nearly three thousand years ago," the Guide had explained. "This was destroyed by the Babylonians but rebuilt by permission of the Persian King Cyrus who had vanquished the Babylonians and taken over their empire."

"Finally," he continued, "It was razed to the ground by the Romans nearly two thousand years ago."

"All that remains is this one solitary wall," he added. "Jews come here from all parts of the world. They recite their prayers and often write little notes to God. They stuff these notes into the crevices of the wall, pleading for help with their problems."

"Are only Jews allowed to do this?" Joseph had enquired.

"No the Jews believe that God is the God for all mankind and if you wish to, you may place a note in there."

Joseph had suddenly felt uncomfortable about writing his note. In any case he knew that the Jewish God might not approve of his request. He had spent the entire day thinking about Dalia, the girl from the bus. He wanted to see her again but he had neither address nor telephone number. All he knew was that she lived in Jerusalem. Now Joseph found himself back at the Western Wall. The open concourse was much busier than earlier in the day. There were many hundreds of Jews there in all the different types of attire he had become used to seeing in Natanya. He noticed that most of them were gathered around tables in small groups and obviously praying in unison. There were just a few actually alongside the Wall. Most of these rested their open palms on the wall as they prayed. As he watched two or three of them made to leave and he was delighted to see that they pushed small pieces of paper into the crevices between the huge stones.

Joseph had picked up a paper skullcap as the Tour Guide had earlier explained and with this somewhat precariously in place he approached the wall. He found a used prayer table and with a small piece of paper from his pocket book started to consider what he should write.

Dear God, please could I have Dalia's phone number? Seemed a bit terse. In any case why should God help him, a Catholic, to get in touch with a Jewish girl?

I have come here, he thought. I am not leaving without at least giving the note a try.

Finally he wrote-

Dear God, I met a girl called Dalia on the bus today. It must have been your will that we met otherwise you would not have let it happen. I would love to see her again. Please will you help me-Your humble servant Joseph Allbarrow.

Approaching the Wall, he read out the contents of the note in a low voice. Then he stuffed the note into a crevice having looked round guiltily to ensure none of the praying Jews had been watching him.

Joseph then made to leave the concourse and was slowly walking away when a voice from behind startled him.

"*Shalom Aleichem* (Greetings)," the voice enquired, "and where are you from?"

He turned to see a bearded man in his late twenties. He was wearing the knitted skullcap that was virtually de rigueur for the Modern Religious Israeli. He was tall and his beard was streaked with a sprinkling of grey hairs. He had soft blue eyes that seemed a little out of place in his tanned and weathered face.

The stranger spoke again,

"Hi," he said, "I am Rabbi Yossi Alvaro but you can call me Yossi. What is your name?" he enquired.

"Oh, me," Joseph stammered, "My name is Joseph Allbarrow and I come from Ireland, from McGillicuddys

Reeks and I am with the UN in Lebanon, sir," he lamely finished.

"Well then, Hi Joseph," Yossi repeated holding out his hand to Joseph.

Joseph took the proffered hand and felt it warm and welcoming.

"I saw you praying at the wall," the young Rabbi continued, "where did you say you were from?"

"McGillicuddys Reeks" Joseph replied feeling a little more confident with this charming stranger.

"Are you Jewish?" Yossi enquired.

"No, sir, Roman Catholic," Joseph replied and then as if to reassure Yossi who was after all, a Rabbi, a man of the cloth he added, "but I was brought up religious and I am a believer."

"I was sure you were Jewish," Yossi explained. "I hope you do not mind me stopping you like this. We get many young Jewish men here at the Wall and they are often in need of both spiritual and practical help."

"Sir," Joseph answered, "I never met a Rabbi before and it is a privilege."

"Joseph, please stop calling me Sir," the Rabbi replied, "My name is Yossi. Everyone calls me Yossi."

Occasionally Yossi's instinct had let him down before and he had approached non-Jewish young men such as Joseph at the Wall. After discovering that he had made an error he had always wished them well and let them proceed on their way. With Joseph however, for some strange indefinable reason, he wanted to prolong the conversation. There was something about this young, raw Irishman that had awakened his curiosity.

"Would you fancy a coffee?" the Rabbi enquired.

Joseph equally felt inexplicably drawn towards Yossi. He was nothing like the priests he had known at home nor did he resemble the imposing and aloof men of the cloth he had encountered in the churches here in Israel. Sure, Yossi was very warm and friendly but there was something more that made him aware of an almost instantaneous bond with the young Rabbi.

"Yes," Joseph answered with uncharacteristic eagerness, "that would be great."

The pair made their way up the steps away from the Western Wall into the first café they encountered in the Jewish Quarter of the Old city.

As they walked Yossi had pointed out various sites from the ancient past of this amazing city. Finally they settled at a table with the most breathtaking view of the Western Wall and the two Mosques that stood on the high ground behind.

"Do you know," Yossi enquired, "that the Mosques are on the site of our Holy Temple, destroyed by the Romans almost two thousand years ago?"

Yossi had heard and absorbed all this information earlier in the day from the Tour Guide. Now however, he had a chance of getting some answers to questions that had nagged him on the Tour.

"If the Temple was…" he thought for a moment, "God's home on earth, why did he let it be destroyed."

Wow, Yossi thought. *That is one question I have never been asked me before.* However, he had an answer.

"The Temple was destroyed because God was angry with our people. They had forsaken much of his Holy Law and were involved in factional strife with each other."

"Instead of fighting the heathen Roman enemy," he continued, "the Jews at that time were too busy fighting each other."

After a pause he continued. "Do you think that God needs Temples, Synagogues, Churches or Mosques?"

"No," he answered himself, "we, mankind, need these places to worship God but that can only have meaning if we conduct all other aspects of our lives in a decent, God-fearing way."

Joseph nodded and had another question ready,

"I believe the Arabs conquered the country some six hundred years later. Why did they decide to build their Mosques at the same place where the Jewish Temple had stood?"

"You, as a Christian must know all about our Bible and the part you call the Old Testament," the Rabbi explained. "The Muslims too, follow most of the Jewish scriptures. We all believe in the same God but have different ways of approaching him. The Arabs recognised the site as Holy and decided to build there"

"There is also the legend of Mohammed, their prophet, going to heaven from there on a fiery steed. However that is just a legend," he concluded.

Joseph was just getting into his stride. Here was someone who gave straight answers to straight questions and seemed to be more than happy to impart his amazing knowledge to Joseph.

"What about the coffee?" the Rabbi enquired.

"Yes please," Joseph answered feeling somewhat rude. *I am invited for a coffee and I start interrogating my host even before he has had the chance to order,* he thought.

"Do you mind me asking you all these questions?" Joseph enquired as they sipped the delicious cappuccino.

"Not in the slightest," Yossi replied, "I am enjoying the chat. It helps me to increase my understanding of people from other faiths by being exposed to your thought processes."

For nearly two hours the pair were entirely engrossed in their conversation, until the Rabbi remembered with a start, that it was time to go to synagogue for the evening service.

"I must fly," he suddenly said, "or I will miss the evening service, do you want to walk with me or have I taken up too much of your leave time already?"

Needless to say, Joseph had enjoyed the encounter tremendously and was only too happy to accompany the Rabbi on his short walk to the synagogue.

Non-Jews do visit Synagogues from time to time for a variety of reasons, maybe to attend the wedding or Bar Mitzvah of a friend or for tourism. It is, however, very unusual to visit a small synagogue for a quick evening service. And to be invited in by the Rabbi is even more out of the ordinary. However, when Yossi & Joseph arrived at the entrance Yossi was quite surprised to hear himself saying,

"Do you want to come in with me? The service only takes fifteen minutes or so. You will find it interesting and I will explain it to you afterwards."

Chapter Thirteen

Settling In

Ireland 1495

Three years had elapsed since the shipwreck. Three years that had seen happiness and tragedy in equal measure. Little by little they had all come to accept that the chances of rescue from this desolate spot were virtually non-existent. They had realised that this land, Eire, the natives called it, was likely to remain their home for the rest of their lives. Jose now realised that without doubt this new home was in the south west of Ireland, a country of which he had had precious little knowledge.

Both stone houses had been built up to a far better standard of habitation. But when Jose surveyed their home, he could not help but let his mind drift back to the elegant mansion they had occupied in Cordoba. Why and for what purpose had God caused him and his beloved family to be cast into this damp and rugged place?

They had food to eat for which he thanked his Maker, with blessings before and Grace after every meal. They had fish to eat thanks to the crewmen from the ship. They had lamb and mutton thanks to his new friends the native shepherds. In fact they were becoming full time shepherds themselves and there was some satisfaction in seeing how their flock was increasing each year. They had also planted vegetables alongside the stone house. Once again thanks to the generosity of the natives they had a variety of seeds and they had quickly discovered in this perpetually damp climate which ones were the most viable. His beautiful wife Rebecca had metamorphosed from an elegant Spanish lady into a small time farmer. It was she who tended the vegetable garden assisted willingly by her daughter Miriam.

Both Mother & Daughter were now attired in dresses of rough homespun cloth, bartered from the natives in exchange for fish. Despite their simple clothing both Rebecca and Miriam always looked lovely. Their exceptional beauty could not be disguised and the hard outdoor life had only served to remove the pallor that had resulted from the twin hardships of the nightmare voyage and the first months in their unwelcoming new home.

It had, however, become a matter of increasing amazement to the suppliers of the fish, the crewmen, how the Alvaro household managed to consume such prodigious quantities. Little did they realise that the yield of the sea was fast becoming an important currency in the Alvaro household. Still, the fish were easy to catch and the mutton and vegetables received in exchange by the crewmen were more than welcome.

On Friday evenings both families made great efforts in their own homes to replicate what Sabbath eve had been like in Cordoba. First Jose chanted the Sabbath evening prayers with his two sons. Then Rebecca lit the Sabbath candles. Next they should have blessed a goblet of rich, red wine but this was impossible. There was no wine available that they could use. Certainly their Christian neighbours had wine for the Mass in their small stone church many miles away but wine prepared for this purpose was not acceptable for Jewish religious ceremonies. However, they could use bread for the Friday evening blessings. Both families had been able during the first year to obtain wheat and yeast from the natives. Thus Rebecca had been able to bake bread by the peat fire in a stone shed they had built alongside the house. Two loaves of bread were then blessed by the two heads of the families in their respective homes in accordance with tradition. In both houses they did their best to create a festive air and usually Sabbath table hymns were sung during the meal. At the end of the meal both Jose & Yitzchak would invite their families to recite Grace after Meals. The ancient Hebrew formula was Nvarech She'achalnu Mishelo. The two Jewish sailors, Pedro & Jaime were invited to attend either the Mendoza or Alvaro table on alternate weeks.

Yitzchak & Jose met every Saturday morning to say the Sabbath prayers along with the other Jewish members of the party. The service always took place in the Alvaro home. There was the Alvaro family, father and two sons, Yitzchak Mendoza and the two Jewish crewmen Pedro & Jaime. Full formal prayers needed a Minyan; a quorum of at least ten Jewish men and sadly that was impossible. They had to make do with the six men available and Jose decided that they should chant together all the normal Sabbath prayers skipping the Kaddish, which could only be said with a Minyan. The heads of the two families comforted themselves and each other with the hope that eventually with the arrival of more baby Alvaros & Mendozas the day would dawn when their number had grown sufficiently to enable a Minyan to be in attendance for their prayers. That was unless a miracle occurred and they were able to leave Eire.

Three years previously, just three months after their arrival their number had increased with the birth of a lovely baby boy, Shimon to Sarah & Yitzchak.

Also at Sabbath morning prayers they had instituted regular readings from the Sepher Torah, which the old Rabbi had died defending. Elazar had constructed a cupboard from rocks and the ancient scroll was gently returned there after each Sabbath reading.

Chapter Fourteen

A Visit from Joseph

The Reeks 1995

Joseph had found every aspect of Judaism and the history of the Jews to be fascinating. Every time he was on leave from South Lebanon he would arrange to see Yossi in Jerusalem. Joseph still had a virtually inexhaustible supply of questions for the Rabbi and it seemed as though the more he learned the more he needed to learn.

After three years, Joseph could have been excused for forgetting his one and only meeting with Dalia. This was far from the case, however. He remembered the encounter as if it was yesterday and when in Jerusalem with Yossi he always searched the faces of the crowds on the streets in the hope of seeing her again. He had never mentioned Dalia to Yossi and by now was very well aware of the Jewish attitude to marrying out of the faith. He often wondered uncomfortably how he had had the impertinence to have placed a note in the Western Wall asking for God's help in an enterprise so totally at odds with God's own will.

Eventually he decided that he must visit his family in Ireland. However, the trip home to McGillicuddys Reeks was not a huge success. At first the family had been thrilled to see him but they had grown apart. Joseph's life was a combination of the creature comforts of the late twentieth century when on leave in Israel and the mind-numbing danger ever present in South Lebanon on his tours of duty. Both of these experiences were completely beyond the comprehension of his family. Joseph had tried to explain the many scientific benefits he now took for granted in Israel. His father Aron Allbarrow objected to him even discussing these things in front of the other children.

"What lazy lives," these people have. "Is Dublin the same?" he wanted to know.

"Exactly the same," Joseph answered. "All over the civilised world people use mobile phones, television, computers, microwave cookers and all the other technology that goes with modern living."

Aron had become furious on hearing this.

"So your family are no longer good enough for you," he countered. "To be sure, we're not civilised. We don't have any of these fancy things."

Joseph tried to soothe his father and changed the subject by telling him about his friendship with Rabbi Yossi.

This infuriated Aron all the more. With righteous indignation he enquired,

"So with all this 'modern' living, the best friend you could find was a Jew. You know quite well that although our Lord Jesus was a Jew himself, it was his own people who let him down."

"Why couldn't you find a nice Christian boy to be friendly with?" Aron continued.

"You are so wrong," Joseph replied. "Religious Jews are God-fearing people who live their lives doing good deeds to others and many of their prayers are the same as ours. The main difference is that they do not consider Jesus to be their saviour or the Son of God."

"I never thought I would live to see the day when my own son was sitting there before me and uttering such terrible blasphemy," Aron shouted, as near to tears as he had ever have been in his adult life.

After these exchanges it was downhill all the way. It took just three days of staying under his father's roof for Joseph to feel completely stifled by the atmosphere. His father was hardly speaking to him and his mother always followed whatever her husband decreed. As for his siblings they were frightened of Aron and felt it better to give their renegade brother a wide berth. Only Alan was interested and at night in the dark, Joseph, who was back in his old bed next to his brother, recounted many stories of life and death in the battle zones of South Lebanon. In the matter of his friendship with a Rabbi, he said very little and of his encounter with Dalia he said nothing at all.

"I must return to Dublin," Joseph had announced. "I have some old army friends to look up and I need to check my orders before returning to Israel."

"There is only one answer for such a wayward young man," Aron said to Mary as soon as his son had departed.

"He needs a good woman."

"He would have married Mary Meadows by now if only he had stayed at home. I did think, what with Joseph going off, that she would be Alan's bride next year," he continued, "But Joseph has been more spoiled than I ever feared what with the army and the Jews. Maybe when he comes home next time we could introduce him to Mary Meadows, she is a pretty young girl and maybe she could get him to put all the rubbish he has learned abroad behind him and settle down back here again."

For the first time in the best part of a week Aron began to look a little happier.

It was a full year later when a letter arrived from their oldest son to say that he could come home in two months time if they wanted him. His father asked the postman to wait while he quickly scribbled a reply telling Joseph that they were looking forward to seeing him. Aron immediately set out to speak to Simon Meadows about his daughter. Simon was delighted to see Aron and even more delighted to hear the reason for the visit.

"I was never too happy about Alan, you, know," he explained. "To be sure he is lovely boy but he is younger than our Mary and I always used to think that she would marry Joseph."

"Of course," he continued, "with Joseph going off like that it was a shock for us all. So is he coming home for good now?" Simon enquired.

"I certainly hope so," Aron had replied, with rather more confidence than he really felt.

"So just send one of the children over to let me know and I'll send our Mary right over," Simon concluded.

Chapter Fifteen

The First Wedding

Ireland 1500

The Alvaro and Mendoza families had settled into their hard, primitive new life with a mixture of determination and resignation. The heads of both families were deeply and sincerely religious people. They knew that whatever befell them was the will of God. Jose often used to remind himself of the ancient Jewish saying *Gam zu L'Tovah,* which roughly translated to "Even this must be for the best!"

Of course, they all had their bad and sad moments when they remembered their past lives in Spain but perseverance had brought its rewards.

The stone houses were now much more comfortable and in the case of Yitzchak & Sarah's home this had been extended to allow for two further additions to their family. Leah their daughter born in Spain was now eighteen years old. She was tall and slim with fair hair and blue eyes. She was an ever-willing help to her mother particularly with the three younger members of the family. Young Shimon was now a sturdy dark haired little boy of eight, with dark brown eyes that could melt any adult's heart. As a consequence Yitzchak had to steel himself to apply very necessary discipline to the little fellow. Then there was Chaim born in 1496 and Esther born in 1498. The younger children, of course had no idea of how different life had been for the family in Spain. Eire was their home and their father was a hard-working shepherd.

Jose and Rebecca's family had not increased in number but their flock of sheep was growing fast and providing the wherewithal to obtain a slowly increasing standard of living.

Their son, Aharon, was now twenty-four years of age and was engaged to marry Leah Mendoza in July. If he was to marry within the faith Leah was only possible candidate. Fortunately the young couple were deeply in love and both eagerly waited for the day when their marriage would take place. There was of course no Rabbi or Synagogue and it was decided that the two fathers would conduct the ceremony between them. A simple marriage contract was drawn up on a piece of sheepskin parchment lovingly inscribed by Yitzchak for his daughter. The Groom's younger brother Elazar constructed the traditional wedding canopy and they prayed for fine weather to enhance this special and unique occasion.

At last the day dawned and it was fine and warm. Bright sunshine shone down onto the Wedding Canopy standing near the Alvaro house in a rocky hollow.

"This is a day of joy and sorrow," Jose whispered to Rebecca. "Do you remember our wedding in the grounds of the old synagogue in Cordoba? You looked so beautiful when your parents led you out to me, under the canopy. And the ceremony and the celebration afterwards were so different to this."

"Anyway," he continued, "you are still the most beautiful elegant woman in the world for me. Whether you are in silks or homespun you are all I could ever want in a wife."

"Are your eyes still working?" Rebecca retorted with a little smile playing on her lips. "Look at the skin of my hands-rough just like a servant girl."

"And I never dreamed that I would be wearing homespun for my son's wedding," she continued, "Still we are all alive and well and today our first born is bringing his bride into our family home."

The ceremony started with the two mothers standing by the bride. Normally the two fathers would have taken their positions alongside the groom but today they were sharing between them the parts of the Rabbi and Cantor. Traditionally both bride and groom would take wine with the respective parents but there was no wine. For the Sabbath, Apple Juice had been prepared and this was also used for the wedding. All the blessings were pronounced and to end the service one of the few remaining glasses from the ship was broken under the heel of Aharon. This ancient custom dated back to the destruction of the temple in Jerusalem and was to remind Jews, wherever they were, that their final and complete happiness could only be achieved when the Holy Temple was rebuilt on Mount Zion.

There were no musicians or musical instruments but the traditional wedding songs were still remembered. The two mothers and Miriam held hands to form a circle round the bride and danced and sung with such exuberance that they almost forgot the poor surroundings in which they now lived. Likewise the two fathers and Elazar danced with Aharon. Pedro and Jaime, the two Jewish crewmen also joined in the dancing and singing. Julio and Bernardo, the Christian crewmen, watched the proceedings with a mixture of puzzlement and amusement. Soon they too were clapping their hands and trying to join in the singing.

There were other guests. Jose had asked Patrick and his wife and children to join them. Since their strange introduction he had become a firm friend to the Alvaros & Mendozas. It was hard to believe that it was now eight years since the shipwreck and as soon as the stone houses were ready for occupation and Jose could spare the time, Patrick had invited Jose to visit him in his home. It must be remembered that communication between the men in those early days was very difficult as the only language they had in common was Latin. With Patrick this was barely understood church Latin and with Jose the Latin vocabulary of international commerce. Just to explain to Patrick that they were Jews and did not eat pork was a gigantic undertaking. Eventually Patrick seemed to get just a glimmer of an idea of the religion of his new neighbours.

"Jews killed Christ," he intoned in Latin and then seemed to realise that this was an offensive statement to make to his new friend.

"Our Lord Jesus was a Jew," he ventured.

"Yes," replied Jose.

Patrick then resolved to enquire about Jews from the Priest on his next visit some six months later. The Priest was deeply anti-Semitic both by nature and upbringing. He was shocked to learn of Jews in the area and warned Patrick to keep away from the Christ killers. Patrick did not know what to make of all this. He knew from church all about the life and death of Jesus but he had also quickly discovered that Jose and his family were kind gentle and generous people. He liked his new neighbours and felt torn between his loyalty to the Christian religion and his feelings of warmth for his new friends.

However little by little Jose started to learn the strange language of his new home. With the improvement in communication came a better understanding of what the two groups of such diverse people stood for. It soon became apparent that what divided them was far less important than what united them. Respect for God and fellow man was the cornerstones of both families existence. And thus, the unlikely friendship grew.

Patrick and his family lived in what could hardly be described as a village. It did however, have a name-Ballymagee. There were just six stone houses and what Jose realised must be a tiny church. Supplies of food, other than their own produce and many other consumables had to be fetched from another slightly larger village many miles distant. Jose had made the trek with Patrick some six months after their arrival and had been disappointed to find that there was very little there that would have improved their life. On another trip a year later he had purchased a donkey and carried back timber for a variety of uses around their home. Much to José's disappointment even in the larger village his enquiries had confirmed that there were no co-religionists to be found there.

Chapter sixteen

Comatose

Israel-Lebanon Border 1996

In two weeks time Joseph was returning home to visit the family, as he had promised. He loved his parents and family but the prospect of visiting McGillicuddys Reeks still filled him with dread. The dark, damp atmosphere of the area he used to call his home was so different to the bright warm sunshine in which he spent most of his time. *Sure there was danger,* he often mused, *but here he really felt alive.* And he still dreamed of one day finding Dalia again.

Joseph was now a sergeant and his duty was still to police South Lebanon. The false dawn of the Oslo Accords was still a cause for a little optimism in the Middle East but there were frequent problems with Hizb'ulla, the most aggressive of the militias in the area. Joseph had been offered the chance to continue his army career in Ireland but to leave Israel permanently without ever having found Dalia was unthinkable. Furthermore he had grown to love the country and its people and his firm friendship with Rabbi Yossi Alvaro continued to blossom. He probably now knew more about Judaism than many born Jews and he was constantly disappointed by the attitude of secular Israelis to their heritage.

March the 6th 1996 was a day he would never forget. He was on patrol just inside the Lebanese border, with three of his fellow UN men, well within sight of the chain link fence that divided the two countries at that point. A rocket fired from somewhere deeper in Lebanon had landed on the Israeli road just as a heavily fortified Egged bus was passing. Had the rocket hit the bus it would have been all over for its occupants. As it was the rocket landed on the road just fifty metres ahead of the direction the bus was taking. The vehicle had been travelling quite fast and although the driver's reaction was commendably fast the bus finished in the still smouldering pothole the rocket had created.

Fortunately the injuries sustained by most of the occupants were not serious but the people on board had cuts and bruises and two people were severely concussed. An Israeli Army observation point nearby saw the incident and an ambulance was called. How it arrived in less than ten minutes at what was a fairly isolated spot was quite remarkable. The Paramedics jumped out of the vehicle and started to unload their equipment. Then suddenly all hell was let lose. A barrage of gunfire from behind where Joseph and his men were patrolling was hitting the road only a few metres from the ambulance.

Just a little more accuracy and the ambulance and crew would be done for.

Joseph's jeep was equipped with a loudspeaker system and quickly he called into the microphone in English and Arabic that this was a United Nations patrol and the terrorists must stop firing at once. This brought no response. If anything the barrage of bullets became heavier. Two Israeli jeeps came hurtling down the track and started to return the fire coming from the brush only 100 metres or so behind Joseph. Joseph who was driving the jeep shot down the path away from the rain of bullets now coming from both sides. Then he turned across a rough track in an endeavour to get behind the terrorists. Judging that his jeep was now only a short distance from the Lebanese men, he once again appealed to them to stop firing.

United Nations patrols had neither the orders nor the equipment to become involved in this kind of situation. To risk his own men, contrary to the terms in which the UN were stationed in South Lebanon, would mean certain disciplinary action. However, he himself was not about to allow the situation to continue. It was quite intolerable to see a busload of civilians, many children, attacked in this way. He stopped the jeep and told Corporal O'Malligan to drive him and the other men in the vehicle, out of harm's way and report the entire matter to the nearby UN post.

"What about you?" the Corporal enquired. "Why are you not coming with us, Sergeant?"

"Corporal, just do as you are told," Joseph snapped.

"Shall I come straight back for you Sergeant?" the Corporal then enquired.

"Yes, yes," Joseph replied impatiently. "Tell Lieutenant Andersen to bring reinforcements and to meet me at this point."

The Corporal revved up the jeep and shot off along the bumpy track with the two men in the rear seat holding on for dear life.

Joseph in the meantime was quickly and quietly following the footpath that seemed to run in the direction that would lead him to the rear of the clump of bushes and stunted trees. There was still a veritable cacophony of gunfire noise emanating from the area as Joseph came nearer.

What on earth am I doing here, he thought.

These guys care no more for the UN than for anyone else who gets in their way. They will shoot me as soon as look at me.

Then he remembered his dear friend, Lars, who had been murdered by such terrorists as these.

That should have made him afraid but instead it re-doubled his determination to stop this attack.

There are probably three or four of these Hizb'ulla guys, he pondered.

The only chance is to make them think they are being attacked from behind by a number of enemy soldiers.

He did not dare to shoot into the bushes. He knew that if one of the terrorists were killed he would be in serious trouble with his superiors.

Joseph had only one idea and the more he thought about it the more pathetic the plan seemed. However, he could think of nothing else and dreaded to consider the growing number of civilian casualties that must now be occurring on the other side of the fence.

Just thirty metres behind where the Hizb'ulla men were in hiding there was another larger clump of trees and bushes. Joseph approached these bushes and lay down flat to squirm his way into the undergrowth. He took out his pistol and waited for a lull in the gunfire. Thankfully this came quickly and gave him the chance to fire just one staccato shot into the air. Immediately there was a reaction and he could hear raised voices shouting in Arabic. Quite understandably they were astonished to find that shots were coming from behind their position. Before the terrorists had time to decide from exactly where his shot had emanated he squirmed through the trees to a different position and fired another shot in the air. This gave the Hizb'ulla men a better fix on where he was or rather where he had been when he fired the shot. But, by now he had once again changed his position and he did not have to wait long for the inevitable response. The noise was deafening. He had fired one pistol shot but they were emptying magazines of bullets into the group of shrubs he had occupied just a few seconds earlier. He shuddered when he thought of how his body would have looked by now if he had not fled that position. A hail of bullets like that would have transformed him into an unrecognisable lump of bloody pulp.

He moved further away, still under the cover of the trees. They had now started to spray the entire shrub area with bullets suspecting quite naturally that they were being attacked by a number of men.

Hizb'ulla had many enemies in South Lebanon and once the initial shock of apparently being attacked from the rear had subsided they would certainly have suspected that a small band of members of the South Lebanese Christian Militia had ambushed them.

He fired again this time on the run and broke out of the clump of trees behind where he had being hiding. Then he heard the sound of a number of approaching vehicles. He could just make out in the distance three jeeps and an armoured personnel carrier all with the markings of the UN. He started to run towards them just as the four terrorists broke cover with their hands in the air. They too, had heard the approaching vehicles and being unable to identify them assumed they were Israeli or South Lebanese troops. The automatic weapons had been abandoned but the fourth man to emerge realised that one lonely UN sergeant had thwarted all their plans. He pulled out a pistol and proceeded to discharge the bullets in the direction of Joseph's running figure. Technically Joseph was outside the range of side-arm shots but just one stray bullet, discharged at a higher trajectory than the others hit him in the rear thigh as he ran. He fell to the ground tripping on a rocky outcrop and banging his head against the jagged stone. That was the last thing that Sergeant Joseph Allbarrow remembered until…

Chapter seventeen

Lost at Sea

Ireland 1508

There had been great joy after the wedding of Aharon to Leah Mendoza. A year later in 1501 had seen further celebrations when Jose & Rebecca's beautiful daughter, Miriam, had married Jaime, one of the two Jewish crewmen.

"This was not the kind of match I had dreamed of for our only daughter," Rebecca had confided to Jose. "Jaime is a sweet, kind man but he is twenty years older than Miriam and has had little education."

"I always thought that the daughter of Don Jose Alvaro would marry a learned Doctor or Lawyer, someone of similar rank," she continued, "but in this strange land we must be thankful that Jaime is at least of our faith."

Later that year had seen the arrival of Jose & Rebecca's first grandchild, a sturdy little boy who they named Moshe after one of José's grandfathers. Yehuda followed in 1503 and Sarah was born in 1506. Jaime and Miriam had also helped to populate this isolated corner of the earth with a boy and a girl born respectively in 1504 and 1507.

By 1508, Jose felt that they had much to be thankful for. It was sixteen years since their perilous and violent arrival. They had food, shelter and a growing family. They practised their religion with just one or two minor problems. One of these was the lack of a Minyan (a quorum) of ten adult men over the age of thirteen. Jose often pondered that with the natural growth of their tiny community it would be only a few years until this situation righted itself.

Domingo, Julio and Bernardo the three Christian crewmen had quit their cave residence some three years earlier and had built simple stone houses in the village. Patrick had been delighted to welcome them and within a year all three of them were married to local girls. They were deeply religious Catholics and even the priest was forced to admit that without the arrival of the Jews down the coast he would not have gained three such acceptable good Christian additions to his own flock.

There was only one difficulty for the Alvaro and Mendoza families that arose as a result of the removal and marriage of the three crewmen. The three Spaniards had stopped earning their livelihood as fisherman. Domingo and Bernardo started to work in the main local occupation as shepherds. Julio, who had been the ships carpenter started to make modest items of furniture for his neighbours and within a short time, was fulfilling orders from other similar villages, some at a fair distance from his new home. Jose could hardly blame the crewmen from improving their own lives but the lack of fish; one of the main foods in their diet was a big problem. Jose went to see Domingo who promised to train both Jose and Yitzchak Mendoza in the finer points of fishing and navigating a small boat. This proved to be much harder and heavier work than it had appeared when the three Spanish sailors rowed and navigated. Even dragging the nets aboard the tiny craft when they were laden with a good catch of fish, proved to be physically exhausting. Jose had to admit that as a middle-aged man, who had previously been unaccustomed to any kind of heavy labour, he was only fit to navigate the small craft. Yitzchak, however, was younger and had not come from such a protected and pampered background as Jose. He seemed to thrive on the activity and soon became an excellent fisherman. It was then decided to introduce Elazar to the nautical prowess required to maintain a good supply of fresh fish, so much a staple part of their diet.

Rebecca watched the development of these new skills in her husband and son with a mixture of incredulity and concern.

"It is one thing to watch you looking after sheep," she told Jose, "but to see you coming home exhausted and soaking wet from these fishing trips, is something else."

"You are making yourself ill and I think you should leave the fishing to the younger men."

"I am really fine," Jose tried to assure her but he knew deep down that his wife was right.

"Yitzchak has now trained young Shimon to help with the fishing" he continued, "that means that with Yitzchak and Elazar we have three fit young men to look after our fish supplies. I will go out with them just one more time and then leave it to them, in future."

"Thank God you have come to your senses," Rebecca told him.

Tragically her relief was very short lived.

The following Tuesday the boat went out with Jose on the tiller, Elazar and Shimon rowing and Yitzchak looking after the nets. It was a bright breezy day quite typical of the month of March in those latitudes. The sun kept peeping out from the white fluffy clouds as they hurried across the sky. Jose was beginning to enjoy this, his last trip and to regret his promise to Rebecca. The sea was calm but the catch was so far, very disappointing. Domingo and Julio had impressed upon them to never venture beyond a series of wooden markers they had floated. These markers were sections of timber that had long ago floated ashore from the wreck. These were tied with stout ropes to weights that sat like anchors on the floor of the ocean. The sailors knew that beyond this point the seabed dropped away violently and as a result there were vicious currents that made navigating a small boat a major problem.

As they rowed they chatted, enjoying the fleeting glimpses of the sun, until they reached one of the wooden markers.

"That's it," said Yitzchak. "We had better check the nets again and see what else we have caught."

Jose still held the tiller while the other three busied themselves pulling the net into the boat. It was unusually heavy and Yitzchak called out to Jose to wedge the tiller and come and help them to pull in the net. However, no matter how hard they pulled, the net still remained under water. It did not seem to be caught on anything as it slowly responded to the feverish tugging. In the past when there had been a good catch the fishermen could feel the movement of hundreds of fish jumping, struggling and cavorting in an endeavour to escape from their underwater incarceration. Now however the ropes holding the net were shuddering violently as the net bounced around under water. It was probable that more experienced fishermen would have realised what was happening. They had obviously caught something much larger and more powerful than just a hundred or so normal size fish. Moreover they were totally unaware of the fact that whatever was in the net was dragging the small boat further and further out to sea. Suddenly Elazar realised that they were now well beyond the marker.

"Let the net go," he shouted, "we are being pulled and we must get back within the safe area."

The other three glanced behind them and could just see the wooden marker bouncing around in the waves that were suddenly building up some distance away, back towards the land. As soon as the ropes holding the net were released they disappeared with great rapidity. Whatever they had caught had made off under water, vainly trying to become free of the captivating mesh. Then they noticed that the sky had darkened as the fluffy white clouds gave way to dark grey rain clouds. The breeze had stiffened into a strong wind and no matter how hard they rowed, two men to an oar, they were fighting a losing battle. The combined force of rough waves, the current and the wind, was taking them further and further away from land and safety.

At least a further hour had now gone by and they were becoming progressively colder and wetter. All their efforts to row back towards safety had been in vain and they no longer had any idea of their location. They knew from the fast setting sun, just showing on the horizon below a skirt of threatening black clouds, that they were being driven towards the south west and the great ocean that lay there.

Back on land Rebecca and the others were becoming increasingly anxious.

"Where can they be?" she asked Aharon who had just returned from shepherding his sheep.

"Look at that sky," she continued, her brow furrowed with worry. "There is a storm brewing and Jose and the others are out at sea."

As if to confirm the condition of the weather a huge flash of lightning illuminated the stone house and was followed with ominous rapidity by a deafening crash of thunder. Just a few seconds later came the rain. It was blowing a gale and the torrent was lashing against the rear wall of the house almost as if it was flowing horizontally. Rebecca was not the kind of woman who wept with little or no provocation. However, in the realisation of the danger her dear husband and son must be in, she burst into tears.

"Oh Aharon," she sobbed, "Where are they? How can we help them?"

"I am going down to the shore to look for them," she continued with a look of wild desperation on her face.

Aharon grabbed hold of his mother and pulled her towards him.

"No! I will go down to the shore. You must stay here to greet them when they return," he retorted with a small, sad and very unconvincing smile on his face.

"Please be calm," he continued. "I would hate Dad to see you so upset."

But he felt anything but calm himself as he ran down the rocky path leading to the sea.

The waves were enormous and the only time he had seen such a wild sea was all those years ago when they were shipwrecked. Then they were in a large sailing ship and even that craft could not survive such a wild sea.

What chance have my poor father & brother in that tiny frail fishing boat, he agonised.

Aharon ran up and down the beach repeatedly dodging the huge waves crashing interminably before him. Soon the tide had engulfed the beach and Aharon was forced to climb up the rocks to avoid being swept away himself. Eventually he reached the mouth of one of the caves that had been their home when they first arrived. How long Aharon stood there gazing into the blackness of the wild sea below, he neither knew nor cared. Eventually he heard a sound behind him and turned to see his mother sobbing uncontrollably.

"We will never see them again," she said. And with a superhuman effort she straightened up and continued, "We must both be strong for the sake of the children."

"What about Sarah? Yitzchak & Shimon were also on that boat?" Aharon suddenly exclaimed, as much to himself as to his mother.

"Do you think I have not thought of that?" Rebecca replied.

"What will become of us all?" she continued. "We must pray as we never prayed before for God to deliver our dear men folk back to us."

"I brought a book of Tehillim (psalms) down with me. Aharon let us recite some together."

Soon they heard voices and the sound of footsteps on the rocky path.

"Oh, Aharon!" Rebecca exclaimed, "Our prayers have been answered!"

Tragically this was not so. Two or three minutes later, Sarah accompanied by twelve-year old Chaim came into view. She was weeping hysterically and flung her arms around Rebecca. Rebecca, despite her own knowledge of the likely outcome of the catastrophe, summoned up an almost superhuman reserve of calm inner strength that she certainly did not feel.

"Come now Sarah. They may well be safe," she ventured, stroking her friends hair to comfort her. "Perhaps they managed to land the boat further along the shore."

And the two mothers and their sons stood almost motionless in the mouth of the cave peering into the blackness until the rising sun despatched the long night to the other side of the world. It was a bright clear day but in all their hearts there was only bitter darkness as they tried to adjust to the almost certain tragedy that had befallen the two families.

CHAPTER EIGHTEEN

COUSIN JACK

BALLYMAGEE 1996

One of the most striking characteristics of the Allbarrow & Meadows families in their original old stone houses was their technophobia. True they had eventually agreed to have electricity and the radio but such devil's instruments as television and computers were totally beyond the pale. Aron used to persuade one of the villagers to use the telephone in the village on his behalf from time to time, to speak to Joseph but the thought of having the instrument in his house was completely anathema to him.

March the tenth was cold and wet. Moreover there was a strong wind that ensured that every person, animal and object in its path was well and truly soaked. Aron had just returned from the hillside where his sheep were grazing. He was literally soaked to the skin and resolved to dry himself off and to change into his other set of working clothes.

He had just finished changing, with his discarded wet clothes making a growing pool of water on the hard stone floor. There was a hard perfunctory rap on the front door of the stone house. This door was never locked and even in the village, burglary was a rarity. If it occurred at all it was usually the result of some desperate miscreant passing through while on the run from the authorities in one of the larger towns. A knock on the front door was therefore not so much a request to be allowed to enter as advance notice that someone was about to pay a visit.

The heavy wooden door creaked open on its rusty hinges and in came Jack Allbarrow. He was known to be a distant cousin of both of the two families in the old stone houses but his great, great, great grandfather had many generations earlier taken up residence in the village and married a local girl. There was nothing unusual about this. Only the first born of the Albarow & Meadow families were expected to stay in the stone houses and perpetuate the strange traditions. Aron was surprised to see Jack. He lived on the far side of the village and how he made his living was something of a mystery to Aron. Jack was reputed to be quite well off and had installed in his home all the devils instruments so despised by Aron. This included the telephone and the greatest evil of all, a television set.

Aron whenever he encountered any of the contaminated members of the two families always treated them with circumspection. Cold courtesy was the order of the day. Aron, by his own standards, was never rude, just careful to keep a good distance between himself, his family and these distant cousins.

Thank heavens, most of these people move away from the area to what they consider to be more comfortable locations, he mused on the occasions when he encountered one of them in the village

"To be sure," Aron began with a suspicious look on his face. "And what would Jack Allbarrow be wanting with a poor shepherd like me?"

"Aron," Jack began with a look of concern on his face. "I have a message for you and not very good news, I have to say."

Aron studied Jack's face and realised that whatever it was his kinsman had to convey was sufficiently bad for him to be showing genuine concern.

"There has been a phone call," Jack ventured.

"Yes, yes and what did it say?" Aron replied, now thoroughly alarmed.

"Tis your son Joseph, he's been hurt," Jack blurted out.

"How bad is it?" Aron interrupted.

"The poor lad is in hospital," Jack continued. "He seems to have been shot. He is alive but from what the message said he isn't conscious."

"Aron," Jack continued, "I am so sorry. If there is anything at all, at all, I can do to help just let me know. I'm sure you know he is in Israel. Do you want to fly over there to see him?"

Aron had been standing during this conversation but now he stepped back and seated himself heavily on one of the hard wooden chairs.

"Thank you for coming to tell me this, Jack," he said, feeling sick to the pit of his stomach. "If there is anything else you can do, I will let you know," Aron replied stiffly and coldly.

"So sorry, to be sure," Jack repeated. He felt uncomfortably in the way and quickly departed to leave Aron to his grief and anxiety.

It must have been an hour later when Mary returned from market. She had had a good day despite the appalling weather and had sold most of her home-grown produce so that her pony and cart was almost empty. She was soaked to the skin but nothing a good rub down and change into dry clothing would not rectify. The important thing was that the day was a success and her vegetables were in increasing demand in the village.

She entered the house ready to tell Aron of her success. She knew he would only grunt and nod. Sometimes he even managed a little smile and that for her was a huge bonus.

Today as she entered the house she saw him sitting there with his face contorted with grief.

"To be sure," she enquired. "What on earth is wrong?"

No one could describe Aron as a master of subtlety in the best of situations.

"Tis Joseph, he's been shot," he blurted out.

"Sweet Jaisus," Mary replied, trying to take in the news. "Is he, is he dead?"

"No," Aron answered, "but Jack Allbarrow says he is badly hurt."

"We must go to him, at once," Mary said.

"Don't you realise woman," Aron answered. "He is in hospital in Israel-the other side of the world. He is not in Cork or Waterford, you know."

Mary suddenly remembered that there was a telephone number on his last letter. This was the letter to say that he would be home in two weeks time. She grabbed the letter pushing it into her rain sodden pocket. She burst out crying and forgetting everything but the plight of her first-born son, she dragged Aron off the chair and out to the pony and cart.

The telephone box in the village was painted green and bore the legend over it, *Telefon.* Neither of them had ever used a phone before. Aron had stood in the box and instructed the priest or a villager what to say for him and Mary had never even entered the strange green box. They knew that they must pay to use the machine but the only slot seemed to be for a card of some kind to be inserted. There was certainly nowhere for coins to be entered that they could see. After struggling for a few minutes, they realised that they were going nowhere with this infernal instrument.

"Where does Jack Allbarrow live?" Mary enquired.

"I am not going to that den of iniquity," Aron replied.

"And why not?" Mary countered. "You yourself told me how nice he had been and to be sure, did he not offer to help?"

"I am not going there," Aron answered becoming increasingly agitated. "If you want to go, good luck to you. They say he has Television in his house. How can we expect the good Lord to help our son if we associate with people like him?"

"Well I am going," Mary replied. "Where is the house?"

"I'll show you and I'll be waiting outside, I will, while you go in," Aron offered totally torn between the anxiety he felt for his son and his strange rigid ideas of what constituted morality.

Minutes later they arrived at a pleasant stone built house on the far side of the village. There was a small garden and while Aron waited in the still pouring rain at the gate, Mary strode determinedly up to the front door. She rang the bell and was momentarily surprised to hear musical chimes responding to her pressure. The door was opened by a pleasant, neatly dressed woman in her fifties.

"Would this be the house of Jack Allbarrow?" Mary enquired.

"And who would be wanting my husband on such a filthy afternoon?" the lady replied, a little suspiciously as she regarded the soaking bedraggled looking woman before her.

"My name is Mary Allbarrow from the old stone house by the Reeks," Mary answered. "Please. I beg of you, is Mr Allbarrow in?"

""Come in; come in," the lady replied. "I know who you are. You are Jack's distant kinswoman. I'll call him."

"You must be Aron's wife," Jack stated confidently, the minute he saw her.

"I am so sorry to hear about your son. We must all pray for him," he continued.

Mary felt in her pocket and produced the soggy letter.

"Could I telephone this number to find out more about our Joseph?" she asked this pleasant amenable man.

"I'll pay you what ever it costs," she continued.

"Never mind that," Jack replied "I'll dial through for you. Do you want me to speak and find out what is happening?"

"Oh yes, please," Mary said.

The first call went to the UN garrison where Joseph was stationed. However they had no information about Joseph's condition. They were, however, able to supply the telephone number of the hospital. Eventually they were connected to the ward. However, the news was far from good.

The shot had only damaged Joseph's leg and after surgery the wound was healing nicely. The problem was that when Joseph fell, after the shot had stopped him in his tracks, he had banged his head on a rock and now four days later he was still unconscious.

Jack handed Mary the phone telling her to ask the English-speaking nurse whatever else she needed to know.

"At least I know he is in good hands," Mary ventured after her short conversation.

"Where is Aron?" Jack suddenly exclaimed.

"Oh he is out by the gate, he did not want to intrude," she finished lamely.

How could such nice kind people be evil? Mary asked herself.

In a flash Jack was outside and almost dragging Aron into the house.

"Take off those soaking coats," he instructed, "and you are both going to have a nice hot cup of tea."

Every evening for the rest of that week Aron & Mary returned to Jack and Ann Allbarrow's house. From there a telephone call was made to the hospital in Hadera Israel where poor Joseph lay. But there was no change in his condition. By Sunday Mary had made her mind up. If Aron would not undertake the journey to Dublin and then on to Israel, she would go on her own. This was her first-born son and she knew she must be by his side to aid his recovery. On the Sunday evening as they made the now familiar trek to Jack's house she raised the subject.

"This has gone on long enough," she started. "Our poor boy is lying in hospital, maybe at death's door. We must go to him."

"And how do we do that?" Aron enquired.

"Do you realise, woman, how far away Israel is?" He continued. "We would have to get to Dublin somehow. I believe that is where the airport is. Then we would have to catch a plane. To be sure neither of us has ever been to Dublin or been on an aeroplane. I have no idea how to go about arranging it all. And who is going to look after the family and the sheep with us away?"

"Let's ask Jack," Mary quickly responded. "He'll know all about that kind of thing."

"Well I'm not going," Aron replied. "If you want to go, you'll have to go alone. By all the saints, I wish the poor boy well but he is in good hands in that hospital. What could we do if we went?"

Mary uttered not another word and they rode along with the silence only punctuated by the sound of the pony's hooves on the hard ground.

As soon as they arrived at Jack's house Mary told him that she wanted to go to Joseph.

"Now don't you worry," Jack replied reassuringly. "I'll have it all arranged before you can say Jack Robinson."

"In fact," he continued after a moment's thought, "I'll run you up there meself in the car. I could do with going to Dublin anyway."

Jack was as good as his word and the following Wednesday morning saw Aron driving Mary over to the village in their pony and cart to start a journey full of the most amazing experiences for Mary.

Chapter Nineteen

The Alvaro family in 1540

An unbelievable thirty-two years had passed since the tragic loss of Jose, the head of the Alvaro clan and Yitzchak the head of the Mendoza family. Both families had been cursed with far more deaths than births. Instead of establishing a strong and active Jewish community in this unlikely spot, the remaining numbers of family members were sadly depleted. Aharon was now sixty-four years old and his hard life had taken its toll. He was thin and bent with a face lined with deep furrows. He had a racking cough and found it increasingly difficult to tend the family sheep. His first-born son Moshe was really the head of the family and apart from his father he was the only remaining male Alvaro with any knowledge of the Jewish traditions that they had brought with them from Spain forty-eight years ago.

José's widow, Aharon's mother Rebecca, had bravely soldiered on after the terrible events of 1508. Always a beautiful regal lady even in her latter years she died suddenly in 1520 in her vegetable garden tending her plants. Her husband and younger son had drowned and her beautiful and spirited daughter Miriam married to Jaime, one of the Jewish crewmen had inexplicably broken her mother's heart by converting to Christianity with her husband and family. They of course lived in the village and had assimilated into the prevailing culture. Despite all this Rebecca always managed to smile and her deportment even on the day of her death, was that of a young woman.

Aharon was now the only surviving Spanish born Alvaro. His wife Leah had died in childbirth in that terrible year of 1508. His sister had abandoned the faith and in so doing had severed her connection with the family. *Thank God for Moshe,* Aharon often mused. *Without him where would we be?*

Moshe had married Esther Mendoza in 1526. She was two years his senior and a young woman of a serious, humourless disposition. They had produced a son and a daughter, Joseph, named after Jose and Rebecca after Aharon's late mother. These two had inherited the positive characteristics of their namesakes and as teenagers were a source of great pleasure and pride to their parents and grandfather.

CHAPTER TWENTY

CHAIM & JESUS

DUBLIN 1540

Chaim Mendoza was forty-four. He was Irish-born but had spent much of his childhood and early adulthood with his kinsmen the Alvaros. As a result he had learned everything that they had the ability and knowledge to impart to him of his Judeo-Spanish heritage. His family had been even more decimated by tragedy than the Alvaros to the extent that he was the sole male survivor. As a consequence he had originally been determined to marry young. But from where could he find a bride? He would only marry a girl who was of his faith but in the only location where a bride might have been found, the Alvaro house, the one daughter who would have been about his age, Sarah, had died of a fever at only eight years of age. Jaime and Miriam in the village had a beautiful daughter, Ruth, but they had converted to Christianity.

After many years of unfulfilled dreams of a wife and family Chaim began to plan on leaving his stone house. He had heard stories aplenty of Spain and of the land of Israel but he knew that the chance of finding a bride in either country was very unlikely. Chaim had never travelled further than the nearest small town and the Alvaros had told him many times that there were no other Jews to be found anywhere in the vicinity. He had heard tales of large Jewish communities in such far away countries as Holland and Morocco, Turkey and Italy but these were little more than fables left by Jose and Yitzchak.

He decided to take the long and hazardous journey to Dublin from where he suspected there might be just a chance of finding some of his own people. If this proved to be unsuccessful he would take a ship to Holland in his quest for a mother for his unborn children.

Both to finance the trip and to remove his responsibility for their welfare, he sold almost all of his flock of sheep at the market in the town. For the first time in his life Chaim was now the possessor of a pouch of gold coins. Chaim, of course, lived alone since his sister Esther had married Moshe Alvaro so all he had to do was to arrange with his cousins the Alvaros to look after his few remaining sheep. Chaim closed the stone house, packed his few possessions including his prayer book and set out on his adventure.

His main method of conveyance had always been by donkey. The sturdy animal had given him years of service but although it was now reaching the end of its working life, it never complained at the hard work it had to endure. The route he took was over the barren black hills that lay immediately behind his home territory. When the terrain became flatter he rode upon the donkey but over the hills he led the poor beast.

Chaim was totally inexperienced in any form of navigation. All he knew was that Dublin was to the north east of his home. Man and beast struggled on together day by day. They were sometimes fortunate enough to be able to stay over night in one of the small towns or villages that were en route. On those occasions Chaim checked into the local inn and managed to assuage his hunger with bread, fruit and vegetables. Often other travellers and well-to-do local people were dining at the hostelry and enjoying meals of pork, beef or lamb but apart from the outright ban on pork, all meat not killed in the Jewish manner was out of bounds for him. It was then that he missed his home where he could slaughter a lamb according to the Jewish method and roast it on the open fire. All this non-kosher meat smelled wonderful but Chaim was determined not to betray his traditions. *Otherwise why undertake this journey to find a Jewish bride?* He conjectured.

Before leaving the inns each morning he would enquire the route to Dublin. Somehow or other he always managed to miss the crude tracks that would have led him directly to his destination. The last remaining member of the Mendoza family only knew that the sun rose in the east so he followed that direction until towards noon. Then he turned his back on the sun to journey northwards.

The journey probably took twice as long as it would have taken a more experienced traveller but it was mid summer and at least the weather was kind being unusually dry and warm. Then he saw spread out before him a huge cluster of buildings and Chaim knew he was at the end of the first phase of his travels. Soon he was riding down the dusty streets passing ramshackle shacks with swarms of ragged children playing in front of and between the hovels. As the streets became more crowded the architecture improved radically. Now he saw large stone built homes obviously the domicile and workplace of merchants and he began to wonder if José's house in Spain might have looked something like this. Finally he saw the sea. A much calmer sea than the one he knew at home. There were dozens of boats and scurrying along on its surface and two large ships were moored a short distance from the shore

It was early afternoon and Chaim felt incredibly hungry. There was a bustling market just a short distance along the coast and he decided to stock up with provisions and then look for accommodation for the night. The inn he found was near the port and after feeding and tethering his trusty donkey in stables behind the building he resolved to bathe and change his clothing. The innkeeper was a large jolly looking man with a red face and piercing blue eyes. He seemed to take an almost paternal interest in all his guests. He quickly arranged for servants to bring a large zinc bathtub to Chaim's room and to fill it with steaming hot water. An hour or so later, duly refreshed, Chaim descended the somewhat rickety stairs to the lobby. Seating himself at a small oak table he ordered a pint of best beer from the servant girl. As he sipped the quite delicious brew he observed other inn guests going about their business and then returning.

Chaim's native language was Judeo-Spanish. This was the lingua franca in his parent's home. He also spoke, almost as fluently, the Gaelic language of his neighbours in the few villages and towns within the area in which he lived. The Alvaro family, once their geographical location had been confirmed, had learned a few words of English. Whatever knowledge they absorbed, they always did their level best to pass it on to their kinsmen the Mendozas. At the end of the day, the English were the conquerors and master of Ireland and although Chaim had never, to his knowledge, seen an Englishman, it was accepted that some ability to communicate with the master race was essential. Chaim could read and pray in Hebrew but the ability to communicate effectively in their ancient tongue was disappearing with each new generation of Mendozas and Alvaros.

It took only minutes for Chaim to realise that the majority of his fellow guests at the inn were English. At first he had puzzled over what appeared to be a rough outlandish language and then he began to recognise certain words.

He was dressed as a peasant, an Irish peasant, but he was tall and always managed to keep his beard well trimmed in the manner of his Spanish forebears. He had dark eyes and anyone taking the trouble to look beyond the homespun rugged clothes would see a man of breeding and distinction. That is not to say that Chaim had ever had the opportunity to use this breeding and distinction on anyone other than his family and his sheep.

Chaim was so engrossed in his study of fellow guests that he was quite startled by the voice behind him that addressed him in pure Castilian Spanish.

"Buenas Dias, Senor," the man said. "Parla usted Espanol?"

Chaim started to answer the man in Gaelic and then suddenly realised that this man was speaking the language that he had only heard before in the two stone houses that he called his home.

"Buenas Dias," Chaim replied switching over to his Judeo-Spanish dialect.

The man continued in his elegantly pronounced language,

"I knew you were Spanish," he continued. "The trimmed beard and the dark eyes, said it all. But why are you dressed like an Irish peasant?"

"My name is Chaim Mendoza and although I am of Spanish origin I was born here in Ireland," he explained.

"I guess that explains your strange accent," the stranger replied.

He was a small stocky man probably in his early sixties.

The stranger stared hard at Chaim.

"Anyway, Jaime," he continued, using the Spanish version of Chaim's name. "My name is Jesus Rodriguez."

Once again Chaim was startled. He had never met an Irishman called by the name of the Christian messiah and he was very surprised to discover that the Spanish obviously saw nothing blasphemous in the use of the name in everyday life.

Chaim held out his rough shepherd's hand and warily shook that of the Spaniard.

"When did your family arrive in Ireland?" Jesus enquired.

"We were shipwrecked here in 1492," Chaim volunteered.

The man's demeanour suddenly changed. A look of incredulity combined with a certain wariness fleeted across his face,

"Are your family Jews?" he asked.

"Si, Senor," Chaim answered quietly.

Most of the Gaelic peasants who were his neighbours had long since accepted and grown to like the two strange Jewish families further along the coast. They knew them to be good and kind, honest and God fearing people if a little distant and strange in their other beliefs. Occasionally a new priest would arrive preaching how the Jews had crucified the Christian saviour. This kind of language was given short shrift by the villagers. As a result Chaim had grown to mature manhood with little or no knowledge of anti-Jewish prejudice. However, the sudden shadows of fear and suspicion that crossed the face of Senor Jesus troubled Chaim.

"I take it that living here in Ireland, you have converted to Christianity, Jesus enquired.

"No Senor," Chaim answered. "We continue, as best we can, in the faith of our forefathers."

"So Senor," Chaim continued trying to shift the subject of conversation to his fellow conversationalist.

"Do you live in Spain and what brings you to Ireland?"

"I am a merchant," Jesus replied still with a look of wariness on his face. "I deal in articles of fine silver that are crafted in Toledo and I sell them to the English and the French."

Suddenly Jesus leaned forward and whispered into Chaim's ear,

"I would like to talk to you privately later on. Maybe we could take a stroll together. Can we meet at the door of the inn at nine o'clock? It will be dark then," he added conspiratorially.

Chaim was more than a little concerned by the suggestion.

Why should this strange Spanish merchant suddenly wish to enter into a conversation with me that necessitated privacy? He wondered.

The man appeared to be a gentleman and was dressed in an expensive manner.

He does not seem to be a villain but why should he be interested in me, in my homespun clothes? He puzzled.

However, to be prudent he resolved to hide his gold coins and to carry a knife with him just in case his companion was up to no good.

As soon as the clock in the hall chimed seven o'clock Chaim left his room and discovered Senor Jesus waiting for him at the entrance to the establishment.

"Buenos Tardes," the stranger greeted him gravely. "Let us walk by the sea. At this time of the evening it will be quiet."

They walked on silence. Jesus seemed to be troubled by his thoughts and struggling to think of the right words to start the conversation. Chaim was equally troubled but by the suspicions that fleeted across his mind as he wondered what this strange Spaniard could want with him. He knew he could have refused the promenade but this Jesus seemed so worried. As they walked Chaim fingered the knife in his pocket and took comfort from his ability to defend himself if the need arose.

They had walked some distance along the coast when finally Jesus spoke,

"I am going to tell you something known only to wife and family. If this information should ever get back to Spain I would be a dead man."

Chaim turned to study his companion's face and now recognised the raw fear that clouded his visage.

"Do I have your word as a Jewish gentlemen that what I am about to tell you will never be repeated to a living soul?" Jesus demanded.

It was so incredible, Chaim pondered. Here is this wealthy Spanish merchant bursting to confide in me, a primitive Irish shepherd.

"You have my word," Chaim replied.

"I was born in the city of Toledo in 1480 so this is my sixtieth year. My father's name was Moise Rodriguez and my mother was from the de Mesquita family."

"Moise is an unusual name for a Christian?" Chaim interrupted.

"We were Jews," Jesus continued in a strangled voice. "But in 1492 when the choice was to convert, leave Spain or die, my family chose to become conversos."

"I was twelve years old at the time and had started to study for my Barmitzvah later in the year. When we converted the priest baptised me in the name Jesus instead of my Hebrew name of Joshua"

Chaim surveyed his companion with ever increasing astonishment.

"But why did you not tell me all this earlier this afternoon when I told you I was a Jew?" Chaim queried.

"My business takes me to many countries but I am only allowed to travel with other businessmen and it is a known fact that some of my companions are really agents of the Inquisition. They are always on the look out for converted Jews or Muslims who are not true to their new Catholic faith."

As if this piece of information had suddenly reminded him of the ever-present danger he looked carefully behind him to see if they were being followed.

"How long do you intend to stay in Dublin? Jesus asked in a suddenly more confident and matter-of-fact tone.

"I may journey on abroad from here but that is yet to be decided," Chaim replied.

"Could we meet tomorrow evening away from the Inn?" Jesus enquired. "There is someone I would like you to meet."

"As long as it is not one of the Inquistadores," Chaim replied warily.

"The Almighty forgive me if I brought one of those accursed men. I have lost far too many good friends to those gentlemen." Jesus replied.

On the way back to the inn it was if a great weight had been lifted from his companion. He talked about his family and business and explained that his wife was also from an old Spanish Jewish family who had converted in 1492. Jesus had one son, Jose who was brought up to know the secrets of his origin. On the surface they were good Catholics. They never missed attending Mass and confession. They wore large Gold crosses in the fashion of the day. They gave generous donations to the Church and marked all festivals and saints days with exceptional piety. That was their public life. In the privacy of their home they still lit candles on Friday evening to herald the arrival of the Jewish Sabbath. They learned and taught each other the Hebrew language and could recite the most important prayers off by heart. However, the possession of books in Hebrew would have been more than enough for the inquisition to have them burned at the stake as heretics. So little by little the rich heritage that had been Jesus' birthright was being eroded away.

Jesus told Chaim that his son Jose had managed to escape from Spain by taking the dangerous journey via the Pyrenees into France. He had then journeyed across to one of the ports in the south of France and gained a place as a deck hand on a ship bound for Palestine.

Jesus and his wife had been sick with fear as to the fate of their only son. After a year they had become convinced that he was dead. This left an aching void in their hearts only partially ameliorated by the pleasure of presence of their only daughter Maria, who remained unmarried at twenty five years old.

Then an even greater disaster had hit the family. Maria had been reported to the Holy Inquisition for eating unleavened bread on Passover. Fortunately, before the officers arrived a friend had warned her and she was forced to flee her parents home.

Maria managed to keep in touch with her parents through Christian friends who were above suspicion to the authorities. This was however no substitute for having their daughter living at home.

Then one day a stranger, ragged and dirty from a long journey, arrived at their home. He told them he was Gregorio Sylvestre, an Italian Christian sent to their home by the local priest. Gregorio certainly seemed to be in need of food and shelter. However, once inside the Rodriguez home, he told them his real identity.

"My name is Gvirol ibn Daoud and I come from the Holy city of Jerusalem."

Dropping his voice he continued,

"I bring you greetings from your son Jose. He is now known as Yosef ben Joshua Rodriguez and he is studying to become a Rabbi."

Jesus and his wife were overjoyed. Jose was alive and well and living in the holy city as a proud Jew studying his own faith.

Chaim and his companion had stopped walking and just stood conversing in the dark near the beach where the noise of the lapping tide drowned their words from even a nearby eavesdropper, had such a one existed.

"What family do you have?" Jesus suddenly enquired.

"I am the last. My own family the Mendozas were all wiped out in a series of tragedies. My cousins the Alvaros have also had more than their share of sorrow but at least with them the line will continue."

"I never married as I had no desire to marry out of the faith and to bring up non-Jewish children. The Christians in the nearby village are nice folk, God-fearing and good friends but their ways are not our ways. We have all learned to respect each other but we marry our own."

Chaim was surprised by the way in which his companion greeted this information.

"Never mind," he said with a broad smile on his face. "Maybe all is not yet lost for the Mendozas."

"What does that mean?" Chaim retorted, genuinely puzzled by the enigmatic reply.

"We will walk & talk again tomorrow night and then I will explain" Jesus replied.

The pair covered the remaining distance to the Inn in silence and with a courteous bow to each other repaired to their respective rooms.

Chapter Twenty-One

The Sleeping Hero

Hadera-Israel 1996

Mary's journey was the most amazing experience of her life. She had never visited a large city such as Dublin. She had never flown in an aeroplane and for that matter even a car journey was a rare happening in her simple life. She found the crowds in Dublin Airport overwhelming; she had never seen so many people in one place before.

Once she had settled down in her seat, generously paid for by cousin Jack and the plane was airborne, she began to relax and enjoy the view. Her main consideration was her son Joseph and how she would find him when she arrived. She prayed to herself fervently as the aircraft sped on its way, sometimes with her rosary and sometimes without. She was seated next to a pretty, dark haired young lady who occasionally tried to engage her in conversation. The girl's accent was English not Irish; she knew that much from the occasional tourists who stumbled, usually by accident, upon her nearby village of Ballymagee. However, with Joseph uppermost in her mind, she was in no mood for a sociable chat, no matter how charming her companion might be.

Usually, the passenger flights from Ireland to Israel involved at least one change, if not two. This was a charter flight and it required Jack's considerable powers of persuasion to obtain a seat for her. However, when he had explained that Mary was on her way to visit her son, seriously injured in South Lebanon, a seat was suddenly found for her.

Most of the other passengers were foreigners, speaking in a language she was totally unable to understand.

Some three hours into the flight she decided that she was being rude and unfriendly to the young lady sitting next to her. In any case she could not help but wonder what was the nationality of most of her fellow passengers? Despite her heavy heart Mary forced a smile and turned to speak to her neighbour.

"I was wondering," she began, "I was wondering what is the language that most of the people are speaking on this plane?"

The pretty lady looked at her a little surprised,

"They are speaking Hebrew," she answered. "Most of the people on this plane are returning members of an Israeli trade delegation,"

"Have you never been to Israel before?" she continued.

"To be sure I have never even been to Dublin before," Mary answered. "My poor son Joseph is lying in hospital in Israel injured and I am on my way to see him. I am very worried about the poor lad," she explained.

The young lady looked into Mary's eyes and saw the anguish.

"Please try not to worry too much. I know you are religious because I saw you with your rosary. I am sure the Almighty will look after him for you and you will find him on the way to recovery when you arrive. How was he hurt?" she continued. "The standard of driving in Israel is appalling. Was it a road accident?"

"No," Mary answered, blinking back her tears. "He is in the UN army and from what they say he was hurt fighting terrorists in South Lebanon."

Her neighbour greeted this statement with obvious surprise and gently explained;

"The UN people only carry very light arms and as a rule never get involved with terrorists."

"I don't know much about what happened," Mary countered, "but they said something about an attack on a bus."

Her companion studied her face and felt more than a little compassion for the poor woman. Israelis know far too much about death and injury not to be able to share the suffering of others.

There followed a few moments of silence with both women lost in their own private thoughts.

"I think it is about time I introduced myself," the pretty lady then suggested.

"My name is Dalia Mendoza and I work for the Israeli Embassy in Ireland," she explained with a smile.

Mary could not understand how or why she felt so close to this foreign young woman.

However, she told Dalia that her name was Mary Allbarrow and proceeded to give her far more detail about her family and life than she had ever divulged to another living person, let alone a stranger.

"And where do you live in South West Ireland? Dalia eventually enquired.

"You will never have heard of it, that is for certain," Mary replied. "The area is known as McGillicuddys Reeks."

I've heard that name before, Dalia pondered and then with a start realised that the young Irish soldier on the Jerusalem bus two years ago had come from there.

Now what was his name? She pondered. *Oh no! She suddenly realised. Joseph Allbarrow! That was his name! So this is his mother and the poor lad is injured.*

Mary observed her new friend and wondered why she had suddenly fallen silent.

"McGillicuddys Reeks," she repeated. "To be sure you've never heard of it!"

Still her companion remained silent. Then realising that she was ignoring the poor woman, but anxious not to divulge that she had met Joseph, she replied slowly,

"I am not sure. I just might have heard of it. But I don't know if I could even pronounce it," she finished lamely.

With that final exchange both women returned to their private thoughts. Little did Mary realise that Dalia was remembering her one and only encounter with Mary's son Joseph and the undying impression that he had made upon her at that short meeting. As the plane landed at Ben Gurion airport Dalia decided to take the plunge and obtain some method of contacting Joseph. Somehow, her long dormant feelings for the young man were forcing her to enquire. In any case, she persuaded herself, this woman is an unspoilt jewel. How often in this day and age do you meet people of such loyalty, religiosity and sincerity?

"What hospital is Joseph in?" Dalia enquired trying to appear as casual as possible.

Mary took a crumpled piece of paper from her handbag and showed it to Dalia.

Dalia nodded, told Mary that her thoughts and prayers would be with Joseph and the two women disembarked separately from the plane.

Chapter Twenty Two

Mario-Maria

Dublin-Ireland 1540

Chaim spent the following day making enquiries about the cost and likelihood of obtaining a passage on a ship bound for one or another of the destinations where he had heard that Jewish communities were to be found. Although Holland had been his first choice, Turkey, the most expensive destination, seemed to offer a better chance of fulfilling his quest to find a bride. He resolved buy a passage from the captain of a ship arriving the following day. In the meantime he had the evening to look forward to. He liked Jesus although the name still troubled him. The original Jesus had no place in the religion of the Jews but even so, the casual use of the name in the manner of the Spanish Christians seemed very much like blasphemy. He knew his Irish Catholic friends at home would be quite shocked to discover such indiscriminate use of the name of their saviour by their Iberian co-religionists.

Chaim resolved to call his new friend Joshua and then began to ponder the meaning of the strange enigmatic comment that closed their meeting the previous night.

Joshua was fully ten minutes late and not alone. A small, slight young fellow who was hooded in the manner of a monk accompanied him. Chaim glanced uneasily at the unexpected interloper and then turned to Joshua for an explanation. None was forthcoming however.

"Good evening Jaime," Joshua warmly greeted him.

He seemed to treat the strange figure at his side as if he were invisible

"I trust you had a good and fruitful day," he continued.

"Shall we walk?"

Chaim felt it was discourteous and inappropriate to interrogate his new friend on the identity of their companion and the strange trio proceeded to stroll along the quayside.

As they walked they chatted about the most inconsequential of matters and Chaim was becoming more and more irritated by Joshua's mysterious behaviour.

Eventually they left the busier area of the quayside and entered an area of darkness where there were no flares to light the way for night time strollers. It was a cloudless night-something of a rarity in Ireland and the only illumination was that provided by the half-moon.

Suddenly Joshua's whole demeanour changed. From a relaxed Spanish gentleman enjoying an evening stroll he ceased conversation almost in mid sentence, straightened up to his full height and turned to looked at Chaim with a hitherto un-characteristic look of desperate seriousness on his face.

"Do you know who this is?" he enquired of Chaim, glancing anxiously towards their silent companion.

"No, of course I don't," Chaim answered a little sharply. He was not used to being toyed with and could not conceive what game Joshua was apparently playing with.

Joshua turned to the hooded young man and murmured something to him in a dialect of Spanish quite incomprehensible to Chaim.

The young man instantly straightened up and threw off his hood to show the quite lovely face of a young woman. Chaim gasped in astonishment and felt unable to speak as he surveyed the olive skin, red lips and dark eyes observing him with a faint smile just quivering at the corners of her mouth. Chaim was rooted to the spot. He had seen pretty young women at home in the nearby village and as a normal red-blooded man had needed the strongest of strong will power to resist trying to make their acquaintance. This woman, however, was something else and Chaim felt an immediate need to communicate with her.

After what seemed like an eternity of silence Joshua spoke.

"May I introduce to you my daughter Maria Rodriguez," he said grandly.

"Your daughter," Chaim replied, "but how, what, where?" he stammered.

"You never told me she was with you," and realising that he had not addressed a single word to the young woman, he continued with a courtly bow,

"Welcome to Ireland, my name is Chaim…"

"Yes, yes," she interrupted, "I know all about you from my father."

Her face was a vision of loveliness and her voice was equally enchanting.

"You are Chaim Mendoza and your family was shipwrecked here in 1492 after fleeing the evil of Ferdinand & Isabella. You must tell me all about your home and your kinsmen the Alvaro family."

Joshua seemed more than content to leave the conversation to his daughter and his new friend. Chaim was a truthful person and in any case had no reason to paint a glamorous picture of where he lived. He told it, as it was, hard, damp, cold and with very few creature comforts.

The three of them had been standing still in the cool night air for nearly two hours when Joshua suddenly interrupted the dialogue.

"You two must be frozen, I know I am. We must return to the inn now or suspicions will be aroused by our absence at such a late hour. You must not breathe a word about Maria to a living soul," he continued, looking fearfully around him. "I know for a fact that there are two Spaniards staying at the inn who look very much like agents of the Inquisition. Please remember one wrong word could put all our lives in danger."

The following day was Thursday and once again the trio set off on an evening stroll. The Irishman was dressed as a peasant but with an almost aristocratic demeanour; the Spaniard in all his finery and the hooded 'youth' appeared to be the Spaniard's servant.

Once they were out of the flare lit area Maria joined in the conversation and the three seemed intent in getting to know as much as possible about each other.

The next evening was Friday, the beginning of the Jewish Sabbath. Chaim had brought oil lamps and a beer-like home brewed beverage with him and had purchased bread from one of the nearby bakery-stalls during the day. He had supervised the baking to ensure no animal fat was present and with these three items, the Beer, the Bread and the oil lights he prepared to say his prayers in his room as the sun sank behind the Dublin hills.

Chaim knew from his father that ideally wine should be used to usher in the Sabbath with the Kiddush prayer but he had never, in his whole life, ever tasted wine. Monks for the Mass in church prepared the only wine that was available in the Reeks.

Chaim had told Joshua and Maria that he would be unable to see them during the Sabbath and was more than a little surprised when there was a gentle knock on his room door.

What on earth can the maid want at this time? He pondered.

He lifted the latch to open the door and observed the strange hooded garb that he knew to disguise Maria. Quickly he ushered her into the room feeling nevertheless that it was hardly proper for her to be on her own with him particularly in a room containing a large bedstead.

"My father said I could come to your room for Kiddush," she explained, "and then I must leave."

"Of course," Chaim assented.

Quickly he filled the cup with the homemade brew and intoned the prayers welcoming the Sabbath. He was amazed to find that Maria, although brought up as a Catholic, knew all the Hebrew words and recited them with him in an undertone.

He sipped the beverage and handed the cup to Maria to do likewise.

"Shabbat Shalom," Maria then said and made to leave.

"My father asked that we meet again tomorrow evening after Shabbat for our usual walk, is that all right?" she enquired.

And then it happened, the door was flung open and two men, probably Spanish, judging by their clothing and appearance, entered with swords drawn. One man held the point of his sword at Chaim's throat while the other picked up Maria, like a bundle of rags and made off through the door with her. The second man, sword outstretched, backed slowly towards the door of the room and then turned to run after Maria and her captor.

As a boy Chaim had indulged in a few fights both with boys from the families and the village but since manhood he had never been involved in violence of any kind. However, his own personal safety was at the bottom of his list of priorities as he hurled himself in pursuit of Maria and her kidnappers.

The main room of the inn was empty and Chaim dashed through the open door of the building expecting to see the two men running with poor Maria in one direction or the other. However, the area was deserted.

Stop and think, Chaim told himself. *First I must tell Joshua what has happened and then together we must search for her.*

Joshua had seemed to be a calm, self-possessed man but when Chaim recounted the recent events he, quite understandably dissolved into tears.

"If they get her back to Spain they will kill her," he sobbed. "She is a known Judaiser and will receive no mercy from the inquisition. My beautiful daughter will be burned at the stake," he blurted out.

There were so many possibilities as to how the men had got away so quickly with Maria. She might still be a prisoner in one of the rooms but as the English controlled Dublin and had no love for the Spanish, this seemed less than likely. For two Spanish men to be caught imprisoning a young woman in the bedroom of an Inn, was asking for trouble. Instead of the Inquisition executing her, the English would cheerfully execute them. No, they must have escaped through the small back entrance used by the servants of the Inn.

"There is a Spanish ship in the harbour," Joshua suddenly exclaimed. "That is where they will take her."

The two men ran to the quayside and sure enough, a small boat was just discernible in the gathering darkness making its way to the Spanish Galleon.

"Now what do we do?" Joshua enquired in a voice tight with emotion.

"How long is the ship here for?" Chaim enquired.

"If it only arrived today it will be here for at least three or four days to discharge and collect cargo," Joshua explained.

"I think I have a plan to rescue Maria but I need to time to consider it," Chaim replied.

"Come inside and have a glass of good Irish whiskey. Tomorrow will be a most unusual Shabbat but I will get her back."

Chaim said these last words with as much confidence as he could muster but deep down he felt anything but sure that he could rescue Maria.

Chapter twenty three

A Bedside Vigil

Hadera 1996.

The hospital was huge. And the crowds of people scurrying in all directions reminded her of the airport at which she had arrived only two hours earlier. There were Arab men; some dressed in traditional robes, Chasidic Jews in long black coats and women wearing anything from the all encompassing Arab robe & veil to tight jeans or mini skirts. Most of the Jewish women were dressed in western clothes but some of them were wearing headscarves or what appeared to be wigs. And then there were the children. Groups of them were happily playing outside the hospital quite oblivious to the searing sunshine and the never-ending parade of adults entering and leaving the large building.

Mary had arrived by taxi and was pleasantly surprised to discover that the driver spoke fluent English with what he had explained was a Russian accent. When she explained her mission he insisted on accompanying Mary into the hospital to ensure there would be no linguistic barrier to quickly locating her son. She found Joseph in a side ward. It broke her heart to see her son connected to an array of wires and tubes but she realised that but for them he would now be lost to her forever.

Joseph appeared to be in a quiet deep sleep and she spoke to him quietly hoping that her voice would awaken him from his slumbers. The nurse who had accompanied her to the bedside had already confirmed that he had never regained consciousness since the incident in South Lebanon. She was able to assure Mary that all Joseph's vital signs and readings were in good order but the deep sleep into which he had been plunged was totally in control. She sat patiently by his bed that first day until an Irish officer from UNIFIL arrived. He introduced himself as Captain O'Hagan and told her of the heroic way in which her poor son had collected such a grave injury.

"I must tell you Mrs Allbarrow," he enunciated in his soft, educated Dublin accent, "your son is a hero. What he did was way beyond what would have been expected of him."

"If the truth be known," he continued, "he exceeded his orders but he saved the lives of a number of people in the most difficult of circumstances."

"The UN is not always very popular here in Israel but when the news of the way that Sergeant Allbarrow had saved the lives of an entire busload of people, hit the news here, suddenly the UN has become much more welcome and it is Joseph we have to thank for that."

"We are all hoping and praying that he will soon regain consciousness."

Captain O'Hagan told her that he had arranged for Mary to stay in a small hotel near to the hospital and he accompanied her there before returning to duty. . Sadly the UN could not shoulder this expense, he explained. However her husband's cousin Jack Allbarrow had insisted on covering the entire cost of the trip with far more generosity than her husband Aron's family deserved, given Aron's sanctimonious attitude towards him.

For the next few days Mary spent most of her waking hours sitting by her son's bedside but she remained unrewarded by even a glimmer of movement from the sleeping young man.

Chapter twenty four

The Master of the Santa Isabella

Dublin Bay 1540

Chaim had been taught well by his father, in the laws that governed the behaviour of an orthodox Jew. He knew that saving a life was the greatest of all Mitzvoth (good deeds.) Chaim strictly observed the Sabbath laws but he knew that all these rules could be suspended until Maria would be safely back with them on Irish soil. Joshua, Maria's father was inconsolable. From the self-possessed, urbane, confident Spanish merchant and man of the world he was transformed into a pitiful being who sat on Chaim's bed throughout the night, holding his head in his hands and repeatedly breaking into heart rending sessions of uncontrollable sobbing. Chaim knew that in the state this poor man was in, it would be up to him and he alone to rescue Maria.

All night, he pondered on how this rescue could be achieved but no simple plan presented itself to him. He must somehow get on to the ship and then devise a rescue strategy.

What excuse could he think of to get aboard the vessel? He agonised.

Chaim waited anxiously for first light. He had tried his best to comfort the distraught father but to no avail. Finally he told Joshua to remain in the room with the door bolted while he went out to make some enquiries about the Spanish ship.

The port office was only a short walk from the Inn and Chaim was pleased to see signs of activity inside the wooden structure. He entered to be greeted by a gruff Englishman who seemed to be anything but welcoming.

"Yes," he barked, taking in at a glance the rough homespun clothing that marked Chaim as a countryman.

"What do you want?"

Chaim had learned some English but felt more comfortable in either the Gaelic tongue or Spanish. He was, therefore, just as direct with his reply as this arrogant official.

"What is that ship?" he enquired, pointing out to sea towards the Spaniard.

"What do want to know for?" the Englishman replied.

"What business does an Irish peasant have with a Spanish ship?" Then with a smirk he continued, "Why don't you go back to your sheep, isn't that more in your line?"

The official was about fifty years old, of swarthy complexion and dressed in a filthy naval style uniform. He was a man who considered himself, with little or no justification, to be the superior of almost everyone he encountered on this dreadful island.

He dealt with Spaniards, Frenchmen, Scots and Dutchmen all of whom he considered to be foreign scoundrels. As for the Irish, they were the scum of the earth in his opinion. The only people he treated with fawning respect were the English ship owners, captains and military personnel. Had this worthy even an inkling of common sense, he would have realised that although the man before him was dressed in peasants clothes and spoke poor English with a heavy Irish accent, there was something different about him and his demeanour.

"Anyway," the official continued after once again surveying Chaim's clothing with unconcealed disgust "If you've had enough of your filthy sheep, the slimy Spanish are looking for deck hands. Maybe they would take you; you seem to be strong enough."

Then with a leer he added,

"That would be one less of you pathetic peasants on this God-forsaken island."

This was just about the best news that Chaim could have received. The insults of such an ignorant man, as this official were not important, getting on to that ship was the only thing that mattered.

"When is the Spanish sailor coming?" he enquired in his slow deliberate English.

"Any time now," the port official answered, "now get out of here and wait for him outside."

A few minutes later a fat, swarthy sailor came into sight, marching along the quayside. Two villainous looking peasants both of whom sported black eyes and cuts and bruises on their bloated faces followed him.

"I believe you are looking for deckhands," Chaim said in Gaelic, being careful to avoid any indication that he spoke Spanish.

"What? What? - I don't speak your outlandish language," the sailor replied in Spanish, waving to him to join the ruffians behind. "But if you want a job just follow me."

Chaim fell into step behind the other two recruits and soon they were in a small rowing boat bound for the ship.

The ship was called the 'Santa Isabella' and was a poor craft with peeling paint on its hull and a rickety rope ladder that the four men climbed with more confidence than Chaim felt for their safety. As soon as they were on board they were marched off to see the Captain.

Mixing with these people who appeared to be among the dregs of humanity, Chaim expected the Captain to be of a similar ilk. He was therefore surprised to see before him a relatively civilised looking personage who he could quite easily describe as a gentleman.

From what he had seen of the ship and the crew, they suited each other but the Captain appeared to be as out of place on this sorry excuse for a ship as Chaim felt that he himself was. When the Captain spoke it was in pure Castilian Spanish and he told them firmly but gently what their employment would entail. The sailor who had brought them aboard then translated the information into a rough English dialect which none the Irishmen could understand. However, Chaim knew from what the Captain said that they were required to do cleaning, painting and maintenance work on board and to load and unload cargo at the various ports they were scheduled to visit on their way back to Spain.

There was something about the captain, a tall aristocratic man, dressed in shabby but clean uniform that made Chaim feel that he might be approachable as a means, if not an end in trying to help Maria to escape from her captors. Chaim also learned from the Captain's address that they were leaving Dublin the following day and would be calling at Liverpool in England as their first port of call to discharge cargo.

However, Chaim's first task was to discover where Maria might be held. He lost no time in exploring the ship but soon realised that apart from one locked cupboard near the galley, he had no trouble in gaining entry to all the crew's quarters and storage rooms. That left just the cargo hold which was only accessible from the deck and the Captain's own quarters. By chance he was put to work repairing the rough timber floorboards of the lower deck and he slowly progressed towards the door of the Captain's cabin as he undertook his task.

He was on his hands and knees when the door opened and the two men who had abducted Maria came out, deep in conversation. Chaim was terrified of being recognised and bent even lower as he hammered another replacement timber into place. At the same time, he was straining to hear what the two Spaniards were saying but to no avail. Surely Maria would not be held a prisoner in the Captain's quarters, he conjectured. The two men had now gone up to the deck. And then he heard another far more cultured voice addressing him,

"Buenas Dias, Senor Mendoza," the voice intoned. It was the Captain.

Chapter Twenty Five

An Unexpected Visitor

Hadera 1996

There was no change in Joseph's condition. He was still in a deep coma and no amount of squeezing and kissing his hand, talking to him, even singing to him, had any effect. Mary was becoming more and more convinced that her son would never awaken. Sitting by Joseph's bed, day after day, was both emotional and physical torture for Mary. Never having been in a large hospital before she felt initially intimidated by the procession of nurses and doctors monitoring her son's condition. They all smiled at her and treated her kindly and after a few days she became used to the routine. All the wires and tubes to which her son was attached were equally intimidating. She gazed frequently at the dials but the digital readings meant nothing to her. Still they retained a terrible fascination.

At night she ate a modest meal at a café near the hotel and returned to her small room. She was lonely and increasingly convinced that her first-born son would die without ever regaining consciousness.

After eight days of the same tedious but unremitting agony Mary had decided that she was achieving nothing by the daily vigil. She had never before left her husband and other children to fend for themselves. She always undertook the daily chores herself and the preparation of a hot meal each night when the family returned to the stone house. The severe mental pain occasioned by the condition of her son was compounded by worry about the other family members. She was tempted to telephone cousin Jack in Ireland to ask him organise her return but how could she leave her poor dear son locked in this dreadful sleep. She resolved to wait just two more days and if the situation remained the same to then make arrangements for her return to Ireland. It was now Monday and she realised with a start that she had not even been to confession in church the previous day. Indeed she had no idea where she could find a Catholic church in Hadera. All the days had blended into one.

It was eleven o'clock in the morning when the door to the side ward opened. It was about the usual time for a nurse to check on Joseph and take readings from all the confusing array of dials. Mary did not turn round to check the identity of the arrival. She was therefore amazed to see the young lady from the plane standing by her side.

"What are you doing here?" She stuttered.

"I realised after I left the plane that I had met Joseph some time ago in Jerusalem and being in the area," the young lady explained. "I thought I would visit him. After all he is a hero."

Mary suddenly remembered her manners and rose to her feet.

"To be sure, I can't remember your name I'm afraid, but would you like a cup of tea or coffee."

"My name is Dalia, Dalia Mendoza," was the reply, "but more important how is Joseph? Has he regained consciousness?"

"No," Mary answered and burst into tears. All the pent up emotion of the last week was suddenly released by this simple question from this charming, caring Israeli young lady.

Mary came from a family where any show of affection was frowned upon. Her own family the Meadows had been much more demonstrative but other than for purposes of procreation Aron never touched or kissed his wife. As a result the children also were denied any physical manifestation of love. When they were small Mary had kissed and cuddled them but always out of sight of Aron. As time went by and the children grew towards manhood and womanhood all this ceased as any evidence of physical contact would be met with stern rebuke from Aron. Then here she was, suddenly being taken into the arms of this lovely young woman.

"Please, oh please," Dalia said, "Please try not to cry. I am sure the Almighty will give him back to us."

Mary slowly regained her composure and Dalia found another chair from the passageway outside the room so that she could sit next to Mary. For the next three hours Mary had company for her tortuous vigil. The two women chatted about their families and although the subject of conversation returned frequently to the poor young man lying in the bed in front of them, Mary felt just a little less pain.

A problem shared is a problem halved, she thought.

It was late afternoon when Dalia suddenly realised that neither of them had eaten anything for hours.

"Aren't you hungry?" she enquired.

"Well, to be sure I am," Mary admitted.

"You go down to the hospital café for a snack and I will stay here with Joseph. Then when you return I will go and grab a bite to eat myself," Dalia added.

"I can't do that," Mary protested. "You only met Joseph once and if he woke up…."

Her voice trailed off.

"Go on!" Dalia repeated in a determined voice. "I just pray he will wake up soon, whoever is here. That is what we all want isn't it."

As soon Mary had collected her purse, replete with the strange unfamiliar Israeli coinage, she left the room. Dalia moved into the chair nearest to Joseph and after just a momentary hesitation she put out her hand and took hold of his still, pale fingers. She sat like that for a few minutes just gazing into his face and asking herself how she could care so much for someone she had met only once, and then some two or three years earlier. Dalia was a caring person and would have been concerned about any living person lying in a coma. However, with Joseph, for some strange reason, she felt as if he was a dear old friend or close relative.

Dalia, in her young life had seen far too much human suffering. She had assisted seriously wounded victims of two bomb blasts when she had been uncomfortably close to them. She had spent a short period in the Israeli Embassy in a pitifully poor African country where the plight of the starving people had broken her heart. None of this was personal, tragic but not personal. Now here she was sitting at the bedside of this young Irish soldier and it felt so very personal. Dalia could hear footsteps, probably Mary, growing louder as they came nearer. For some unaccountable reason, as Dalia stood up to vacate Mary's chair she planted a soft, gentle kiss on Joseph's forehead.

Full of uncharacteristic embarrassment at what she had just done she quickly resumed her own chair. She turned round to greet Mary with a smile as she entered the room.

They both were startled by the sudden sound. It came from such an entirely unexpected source. It sounded like a groan but what ever it was it came from the direction of the bed. The two women turned to bend over the prostrate figure and were amazed to see first one eye and then the other slowly open and the tiniest suggestion of a smile flicker around Joseph's lips.

Chapter Twenty Six

A Plan

Dublin Bay 1540

Chaim rose slowly from his kneeling position on the floor. He was absolutely certain that he was looking disaster in the face. He expected two or three of the Captain's crew to arrive at any minute to seize him and throw him into a lock-up. He plucked up courage to look into the captain's face and was amazed to see he was smiling.

"So, Senor Jaime Mendoza," he said quietly, "to what do we owe the pleasure of your company on board?"

Not surprisingly he had used the Spanish version of Chaim's name but the form of address was hardly one that would be directed at someone about to be apprehended as a stowaway.

He is just playing with me, Chaim suspected. *Any minute now he will show his true colours and I will be lucky if I do not end up at the bottom of Dublin bay.*

"I needed a job," Chaim stammered in Spanish, completely forgetting that he was supposedly a simple Gaelic speaking Irish shepherd.

Then he bethought himself, *if he knows my name obviously he knows my origin.*

Then the Captain spoke again, this time smiling broadly,

"No more discussion out here, come into my cabin and we will talk properly," he whispered, "You are not the only one with secrets, you know!"

Once they were in the large cabin the Captain seated himself behind a large wooden desk and gestured for Chaim to sit opposite him.

"Now Senor," the Captain began, "I think we both owe each other a few explanations. My name is Alfonso Gomez and I was born into an old aristocratic Catholic family in Castile. I had many good friends among the wealthy merchants in the area. A considerable number of them were converted Jews; Conversos, we called them.

"Some years ago I lost all my money as a result of Moorish pirates hijacking a cargo of spices from the orient. This was just off the coast of Malta. I had mortgaged my entire estate to buy this cargo which would have set up my family, for another two or three generations, but sadly instead I was financially ruined. Three of my Converso friends were about to set up a fund to save me from losing my estate when they were all arrested by the inquisition.

"They were accused of Judaising although from what I knew of them they were all good Catholics."

"So Senor Mendoza," Captain Gomez explained, "the family estate was lost, my wife returned to her parents in Aragon and I, through the good offices of a friendly ship owner, became a ship's captain."

"I hate and curse the Inquisition every day. They tortured and killed my friends who would have helped me to recover my prosperity. Whoever called them the Holy Inquisition? A better description would be the Evil Inquisition. I have witnessed the terrible wicked pain they inflict on people and I have seen too many good men and women burned at the stake. What connection this can have to the God of love is beyond me. "

"I am still a good Catholic and my family have been good Catholics going back hundreds of years. I will remain true to the teachings of Jesus until I die but as for the church that supports such wickedness, I am better off sailing the high seas and saying my prayers privately every day."

Chaim sat spellbound listening to the outburst. After a moment he plucked up courage to say,

"How do you know my name?"

Before Captain Gomez could answer Chaim spoke again, this time urgently.

"Do you know that the two men who visited you just a few minutes ago are agents of the Inquisition?" Chaim enquired.

"Yes," replied the Captain. "They are two thugs employed by the Inquisition to bring back run-away converted Jews and Muslims for trial and torture."

"As for you," the Captain continued with a little smile, "I guessed who you were as soon as I saw you. You do know that I am guarding a very special prisoner in my quarters for these ruffians to take back to Spain, don't you? How on earth otherwise could I know your name?"

The Captain rose from the desk and slid a heavy bolt across the door through which they had entered the main outer cabin. Then with just three strides he was at a smaller door, which he flung open.

"Senorita, come in here, there is someone I want you to meet," he called.

And there she was, Maria, looking as lovely as the first time he had seen her, just one day and seemingly a lifetime earlier.

Chaim rose as with a voice heavy with emotion said,

"Are you alright?"

"Yes," she answered. "Captain Gomez has been more than kind. If only all Spaniards were like him," she said.

"Once I knew I could trust him I told him all about my father and about you, Senor Mendoza. He understood only too well how deeply distressed you would be by my capture."

Maria had initially been locked up in the hold of the ship. The Captain had demanded to see her and gave her captors the impression that he would keep her in his cabin and use or abuse her as he saw fit until the ship returned to Spain. This seemed to impress the scoundrels who probably had something similar in mind as their own treat. However they knew that with such a prize as Maria handed over to the Inquisition on their return to Spain, the financial rewards would enable them to buy the services of many women, far more experienced than the little Jewess.

The problem was how to get Maria and Chaim off the ship and safely back on to Irish soil. The trio discussed various options for some time until it was realised that other members of the crew would be looking for Chaim. That problem was easily resolved by the Captain leaving Chaim and Maria together, locked in his cabin, while he went on deck to tell the first mate that he had put Chaim to work cleaning and repairing his quarters.

Most of the crew had been allowed shore leave and the Captain told the pair of fugitives that he would distribute extra rations that night, of the rough brandy that Spanish sailors imbibed copiously. By that means they hoped to escape from the ship without being seen while the sailors were sleeping off the results of the heavy drinking. It was decided that the Captain would feign an attack on his person once the pair were safely away. The three of them waited anxiously and impatiently for night to fall over Dublin bay.

CHAPTER TWENTY-SEVEN.

RECOVERY AND ROMANCE

JERUSALEM 1996

The hospital insisted on keeping Joseph under their supervision for another three days. However, he had made a remarkable recovery, once he had regained consciousness and the doctors were eventually happy to release him. His mother and Dalia collected him in the latter's Subaru. While still in the hospital the authorities there had kept the press at bay but once word went round that he was well enough to leave he was greeted at the entrance by a gaggle of reporters and photographers.

Captain O'Hagan had authorised him to make a short press statement and after reading this he was led down to Dalia's waiting car. Joseph had intended to return to his billet and relax there for a few days before resuming duty. His Commanding Officer would have none of this and insisted on Joseph taking a month's leave. In addition a number of the Israeli families, whose relatives had been saved by Joseph's heroic stance, insisted on him being accommodated in one of the best hotels in Jerusalem at their expense.

Moreover the newspapers were full of the news of his recovery and Mary felt more than happy to return to Ireland just two days later. Once she knew her son was really out of danger she relaxed and enjoyed her last few days in Israel.

Mary and Dalia had formed a firm friendship and with Joseph relaxing by the hotel pool, Dalia treated Mary to a comprehensive tour of Jerusalem.

When the time came to leave, Dalia drove Mary and Joseph to Ben Gurion Airport.

"Now listen to me," Mary said to Dalia, "we will be wanting you to visit us in McGillicuddys Reeks and I won't be after taking no for an answer."

Dalia took the Irishwoman's hands in hers and promised to come as soon as possible.

Dalia knew that the feelings she had for Joseph were stronger than ever and in his own reserved way she could see that these feelings were reciprocated.

Why, oh why? She pondered; *did she feel so much at home with these people?* She knew Ireland and the Irish. She had worked in the Israeli Embassy in Dublin for long enough. The Irish were lovely friendly people but this family seemed to be indefinably different and their thought processes and attitudes seemed so much more akin to her own. They even looked Jewish she managed to convince herself. She was sure this was just self-delusion to justify her growing relationship with Joseph but so be it, she decided, giving in to the strong attraction he held for her.

Joseph had always considered his mother to be a quiet woman living in the sober shadow of his father. He knew that nothing in this wide world could have persuaded Aron with his simple but fanatical faith to leave the area of McGillicuddys Reeks. He admired his father's devotion to the Catholic religion. Liking him, however and having any kind of warm relationship with him was impossible. He therefore appreciated, all the more, his mother's visit. He did not know whether it was the presence of Mary or Dalia or both of them together that had awakened him from his deep sleep. He did know that it must have been very difficult for Mary to disobey the wishes of her husband, spoken or unspoken and he realised how much he valued her visit and loved and valued her.

As for Dalia, her return to his life seemed like a miracle. He had long since guessed why she had avoided any further contact with him. Indeed his friend Rabbi Yossi Alvaro had explained many times and at considerable length why intermarriage was completely taboo, unless the non-Jewish partner had been properly converted first by an orthodox Rabbi.

There had been daily phone calls during his stay in hospital from Yossi who was in America raising funds for Jewish education. These messages had all been handed to Joseph when he had regained consciousness. Now Joseph looked forwarded to renewing the friendship when the Rabbi returned.

Almost a week had now passed by since Mary had returned to Ireland. Dalia had met up with Joseph in his favourite café in the Old City. This had become a daily routine but this time she had news.

She quickly broached the subject as she had just received instructions to return to the Israeli Embassy in Dublin rather than continue in her new post at the Foreign Ministry. This was a promotion and she knew she must accept it with enthusiasm and alacrity.

"Joseph," she had said, after explaining her new enforced absence from Israel, "You have anther ten days of leave, why not fly back to Ireland with me and visit your parents and family. I am sure your father in particular and your brothers and sisters will be thrilled to see you and it would be a lovely surprise for your mother."

"Why not?" Joseph had responded after just a moment's thought. "I will have to get permission from my Commanding Officer just in case I am needed for some emergency over here."

"However," he continued, "The Reeks are like nowhere else that you will ever have visited. And the old stone house is like something from a bygone age-and that is just what it is, from a bygone age."

And so, just two days later, the pair embarked on a simple journey that would change their lives and those of Joseph's family in ways they could never have imagined.

Chapter Twenty Eight

The Marooned Captain

Dublin-Ireland 1540

By nightfall the good ship Santa Isabella, a shabby hulk on the exterior but a model of good seamanship aboard, resembled a particularly rowdy dockside tavern. The crew could hardly believe their eyes when they saw the barrels of Brandy. The 'old man,' as they called the captain would normally allow one barrel of the strong, rough spirit to be imbibed each night when they were in port. Tonight they were provided with no less than six barrels. As the fine clean-living men that most of these scoundrels were, they had lost no time in sinking prodigious quantities of the liquor and deck was becoming more and more to resemble a battlefield. There were bodies lying all over the wooden decking, often in filthy vomit, some moaning and all less than useless for any duty they might have been called upon to perform.

There were still a few hardy souls who had miraculously remained on their feet. They were lurching around the deck, mostly in twos, singing bawdy ballads in raucous voices or fighting each other. The captain was half horrified and half delighted to see how well his plan had worked. He swiftly returned to his quarters below deck and gestured to his two unwilling guests to follow him.

Stepping gingerly over the crewmen's bodies they had only one serious incident. One of the few sailors still standing had spotted Maria and clumsily tried to embrace her. No doubt the embrace would soon have deteriorated into a rape but with her two escorts nearby, Maria was quickly extricated from her predicament.

Captain Gomez had little or no respect for the Officers of the Inquisition and had assumed they would partake of his liquid largesse along with the crew. However, this was his miscalculation. Just as he was reminding Chaim to rough him up before joining Maria in the boat below they heard a shout coming from the hatch that led to the quarters below deck. It was one of the Inquisition Officers.

"Captain," the voice shouted as much in puzzlement as in anger, "what are you doing? Where is our prisoner? Your door is unlocked."

Without waiting for his confederate he started to make his way towards them stepping over the bodies of the crewmen lying inert on the deck. He was almost upon them when he tripped over a writhing body. Captain Gomez used the interruption to quickly make, in a split second, the decision that would change his life.

Turning to Chaim he said,

"Quickly, go down to the boat. I am coming with you."

Fortunately Captain Gomez always carried a money-belt on his person and this contained a considerable sum in gold coins. Some of this money was his but much of it was the result of the sale of cargo at their previous port of call. However, there was no time to divide up the money and his decision on this would have to wait until all three of them were safely back on Irish soil.

As they rowed away from the Santa Isabella they could hear the shouts of anger emanating from both of the Inquisition Officers. They were hanging over the edge of the deck and now knew for sure that they had, with the active help of the Captain, lost their prize prisoner. Moreover, neither of the men could swim and without the boat they were as marooned on the ship as the captain was about to be on the island of Ireland.

Chapter Twenty Nine

Rory O'Hara's Renegades

Ballymagee 1600

From 1594 to 1603 Ireland was engulfed in the Nine Years' War, also known as Tyrone's Rebellion. This originated in Ulster but gained the support of Gaelic lords throughout the country. However in such remote parts of the island as McGillicuddys Reeks the war had little effect on the day to day lives of the people until the warlord Rory O'Hara and a small group of his men arrived in the nearby village. They were fleeing from a detachment of English soldiers and set about pillaging food and supplies and treating the local people as if they, not the English, were an occupying force.

Fifty years earlier Captain Gomez had arrived in Ballymagee accompanied by Chaim, Maria and her father Joshua. The latter had been in the most terrible state when the three fugitives from the Santa Isabella had found him in the hotel. He was convinced that he would never see his daughter again and was overjoyed to have her restored to him at the inn. After the tears and embraces between father and daughter were finally over, Joshua had been introduced to Captain Gomez. He was a little suspicious of the aristocratic Spaniard but it was quickly explained to him that he owed everything to this gentleman.

"Come on now, Joshua," Chaim had told him. "We will tell you the full story after we leave Dublin. Otherwise we will have the Inquisition Officers after all four of us this time."

With his beloved daughter safe and sound Joshua had quickly regained his normal composure and having paid the innkeeper generously for their board and lodgings they had made their way south-west towards Kerry and the Reeks.

On the journey to Dublin Chaim had often ridden astride his donkey but now with a party of four it took the poor beast all of its time and effort to carry all their belongings. Fortunately Captain Gomez's sense of direction was rather superior to that of Chaim and they arrived back with few mishaps.

Captain Gomez had decided to remain in the village of Ballymagee and had paid some of the local villagers to construct a more suitable home for him than most of those around him. As for the gold that was not his property, there was no way to return it to its rightful owners and as a good sincere Christian he had decided to give it to the church to help the poor. He was however, left with more than enough gold of his own to finance him for the remainder of his now modest lifestyle.

The captain was quickly accepted by the sons and daughters of the villagers who had some fifty years earlier taken the three Christian Spanish sailors into their midst. Domingo, Julio and Bernardo had long since passed away but their children and grandchildren still had a smattering of the Spanish tongue. Once he had made their acquaintance they were certainly very helpful in smoothing his integration into the community of simple shepherds and artisans. Although a middle-aged man Alfonso Gomez had taken a new wife, a granddaughter of Julio and when he passed on there were three new residents of the village with the name Gomez.

Not surprisingly, Chaim had married Maria. This was in a somewhat more simple ceremony than the first Jewish wedding at the old stone house exactly fifty years earlier, when Aharon Alvaro had married Leah Mendoza. Sadly their tiny community was more depleted now than ever.

Little by little the knowledge of their Jewish heritage was being worn away by time, death and ignorance. By the time Rory O'Hara's renegade band had arrived in the area in 1600 the two families knew they were Jews but what that entailed other than in the form of the most simple observances they had little idea.

CHAPTER THIRTY

THE MARAUDERS

BALLYMAGEE 1600

It was, however, still the practice of the men of the Mendoza family to attend Sabbath prayers at the Alvaro stone house. They always took out the ancient Sepher Torah (scroll of the Law.) One hundred years earlier their ancestor Jose had been more than capable of reading the Hebrew script. Even after the return of Chaim Mendoza in 1550 with his new bride Maria, there were members of both families who could, albeit with some difficulty, manage to haltingly read the ancient script. However, by then, the knowledge of the meaning of the words was lost and it was only by passing down stories from the Bible that in 1600 any idea at all about their heritage was retained.

The Alvaro family consisted of yet another Joseph, named after his ancestor Jose, his sister Rebecca, similarly named after the first Rebecca and Yitzchak. Joseph had married Mary (Miriam) Mendoza, granddaughter of her namesake from 1550. Rebecca was betrothed to Aron Mendoza and the future seemed to be assured with a number of other siblings in both families and their respective offspring. They had, in fact been blessed with a number of children and those under ten years of age totalled nine.

It was August and the weather in that corner of Ireland was unusually warm. The year had gone well for the families and sales of their home-grown produce and young lambs at the market had been unusually successful. It was Sabbath and as usual both families had assembled for morning prayers at the Alvaro house. They had just taken the ancient scroll (the Sepher Torah) out of its cupboard and although there was no longer even one male member able to read the holy script, they still laid it lovingly on the dining table and commenced what the children took to be readings from an ancient, tattered leather bound bible that had miraculously survived the original shipwreck in 1492.

In truth although they were all, except the youngest children, capable of reading the Latin script in which the Irish, Spanish and English languages were written, the bible was written in Hebrew, like the scroll, but with a Spanish translation, that none of them understood. As a result they were reliant on their excellent memories of the stories passed down from generation to generation, about all the main characters in the Hebrew bible.

This ancient book was also a chronicle of the history of the two families from the time in 1492 when they had arrived in Ireland. This tradition had been started by Jose and punctiliously continued by subsequent generations until that time.

Suddenly there was a hammering at the door of the stone house and young Patrick Gomez bounded into the room. He was in a highly agitated state.

"O'Hara and his men are on their way to village," he blurted out.

"Who are they?" Joseph demanded.

By this time knowledge of the Spanish language had all but disappeared in the two families. The older members had just a few words but their mother tongue was Irish Gaelic. This was the only language spoken in the south west of Ireland among the sparse population of shepherds and village dwellers. There were just a handful of literate people and this included the priests who had some knowledge of English. As long-term conquerors the ruling power was universally detested. The local people always greeted reports of the battles won by the poor ill-equipped Irish forces further north, with great rejoicing.

In Ballymagee, the local village, they had heard terrible tales in the last two or three days of the behaviour of O'Hara and his men. The villagers were hard put to believe these stories. Had it been the English behaving in this way; that would have been totally credible. The idea that Irishmen would attack their own kin was unimaginable. However, they hoped and prayed, just in case there was any credence in the reports, that the renegade band would by-pass the village.

The Albarow and Meendow families, as the locals now called their strange neighbours, only visited Ballymagee when the necessity arose and no member of the families had had cause to make the trip since the previous Monday. As a result they had never heard of Rory O'Hara let alone of the dreadful crimes he was rumoured to have committed.

"Some folk in the village say they are even worse than the English," Patrick explained. "They could rob us of all our food, burn down our homes and kill all who get in their way."

"To be sure, I have even heard of them running off with the young girls to have their wicked way with them."

"My Mam sent me to warn you and to ask if I could stay here until they have gone."

"Of course you can Patrick," Joseph answered looking deeply troubled.

If they go to Ballymagee and they hear that there are Jews living just down the coast, he pondered, *they will be here in no time. If they treat their own people like that, what chance is there for the likes of us?*

"Thanks to dear Patrick here, we have a chance to hide," Joseph spoke, as positively as he could. Deep down he felt sure that if O'Hara arrived at the stone houses, they would all be slaughtered.

"Come now, we have work to do."

"Chaim and Yitzchak," he said, addressing the senior members of the two clans, "go to the vegetable plots behind the house and dig up all the lettuces and carrots. Take all the women and children with as much food as you all can carry down to the old caves near the sea."

"Aharon," he continued, addressing his fourteen year old son, "come with me into the furthest part of the vegetable garden."

The pair quickly grabbed large shovels as they made their way down to the designated spot.

"We must dig a deep hole," Joseph explained, "deep enough to take the old lead-lined chest from the house."

Aharon was puzzled but too much in awe of Joseph to question him. When the hole was deep enough Joseph went to fetch the old chest.

"Now do you know why we are doing this?" he enquired.

"You are going to hide something in case O'Hara comes," Aharon answered him.

"Whatever may or may not happen to us I know we must protect the Holy Scroll so we will bury it here," Joseph explained. "The lead will protect it from damage."

"You know the names of all the family members, when they were born and when they died are written in the back of the bible. That will be buried as well."

"I always knew something like this could happen. Believe me I have had this plan ready for years."

"You see those flagstones over there, Aharon?" Joseph explained.

"They are very heavy so do not try to move them but tilt the top one and tell me what you see."

"It is all written in Hebrew," Aharon exclaimed. "You know I can't read that."

"Neither can I but I know what it says." Joseph replied.

"It says something that I copied from the back of the old bible. I believe it was written by my Great Grandfather *Zot HaTorah asher sam Moshe lifnei Bnai Yisrael.* Do you know what that means?"

This time Aharon was much quicker off the mark.

"I know we say this when we lift up the Torah scroll before we start the bible readings. It means something like *this is the Torah that Moses brought before the people of Israel."*

"Right," Joseph briskly instructed his son, "go and bring the Torah scroll and the old bible from the house and hurry. I feel that we have little time to lose."

The ancient scroll was lovingly placed in the chest together with the family bible and the chest was closed. Joseph took great care to ensure that the lid was firmly in position so that the contents would be protected from cold and damp.

The pair then set to, to pile pebbles and small stones on top of the closed container until the hole in the ground was covered almost to the level of the surrounding rocky earth. Next they manoeuvred the engraved flagstone so that it covered the area. Then the other four flagstones were placed two on either side of the centre one. Finally they brushed dried earth and vegetation over the stones. When they had finished it was impossible to distinguish where they had been working from the rest of the surrounding land.

Please God, Joseph thought, *when all this is over we could return and dig up the chest with its holy contents. If we don't return then I hope and pray that one day someone will find it and learn of our story.*

The other men in the meantime had been carrying down to the caves as much food and clothing as they could manage and by the time Joseph and Aharon arrived at the cave a substantial store had been created deep inside the dark, dank interior. They all ate frugally that night and the children, to whom this was all a great adventure, were soon fast asleep.

The following morning Joseph and Yitzchak resolved to travel towards Ballymagee to ascertain if there had in fact been any trouble. They were just half way there when they heard the sound of approaching footsteps and hid behind some of the low stunted bushes that somehow managed to grow in this rough inhospitable terrain. The footsteps grew louder until the two were able to recognise six men and three women from the village. They were deeply agitated and running as best they could although obviously completely exhausted and panting loudly from the exertion. Then the reason for the agitation became only too obvious. Not far behind and gaining on the group was a band of some twenty ferocious looking men. These men carried a variety of weapons and looked as if they would use them on the villagers without compunction or compassion.

Turning to Yitzchak he whispered, "Get back to the cave and warn the others. They must not venture out in any circumstances."

"What about you?" Yitzchak enquired anxiously.

"I will stay and see if I can help our poor neighbours," Joseph answered.

"For the sake of your family, please be careful to stay out of sight," Yitzchak replied and was gone.

Joseph was not a violent man. He had also never considered himself to be a brave one. What possessed him to do what he did will always remain a mystery. As soon as the villagers had staggered past, Joseph rose from his crouching position. Hearing the marauding gang getting closer he just stood and waited in the middle of the rough strewn path until they were almost upon him. The situation was totally bizarre. On the one hand there were these twenty renegades, armed to the teeth and in hot pursuit of the terrified villagers and blocking their path was one tall, unarmed man. The gang as one halted in their tracks. Joseph was wearing his usual simple shepherd's clothing but there was something about those dark eyes that made the group suddenly feel uncomfortable.

After surveying Joseph in silence for a full minute or more the leader spoke.

"Who the hell are you?" he enquired. This was totally uncharacteristic behaviour in itself for the O'Hara gang. They were not strong on manners and introductions and killed, robbed, raped or wounded their victims without the niceties of enquiring as to their identity.

"My name is Joseph Albarow," was the reply.

"And what is the likes of you doing, blocking our path?" the renegade enquired.

"You are not from these parts," Joseph replied. "I should be after asking you what you people are doing here."

In the meantime the villagers had fled further away across the hills where with their local knowledge they were able to hide.

"We are part of the army of his Honour Rory O'Hara who is here to protect the good Irish people from the cursed English," was the reply.

"Then why are you chasing my good friends and neighbours from Ballymagee?" Joseph countered.

"They are all traitors to Ireland," was the explanation. "They refused to look after us when we arrived in their stinking village and they have to be punished."

Suddenly a look of pure evil flashed across the spokesman's face.

"Through you we have lost them and you will pay for this."

"You call them your neighbours so where are you from?"

"I am a simple shepherd who lives in the hills here," Joseph replied. Now that the conversation had taken such a turn for the worse he could feel his stomach churning as he faced up to the gang.

"I know who you are," the leader continued. "You are one of those accursed Christ killers, the Jews who, we heard tell, live round these parts."

"He crucified Christ so let's crucify him."

The dialogue was at an end and although Joseph had enabled his neighbours to escape he was about to pay the penalty for his actions.

When Yitzchak had returned to the cave and told the others what was happening it was resolved that the six grown men from the families together, with Patrick Gomez, would return to search for Joseph. Young Aharon had wanted to accompany them but he was instructed to remain in the cave to help the three women to look after the younger children.

When the six men of the families and young Patrick crept up to where Yitzchak had left Joseph they were horrified to see their dear kinsman nailed to a tree with daggers through his wrists and ankles. As they gaped in horror at the scene they suddenly heard raucous laughter coming from behind where they stood. Within seconds they were surrounded by a group of the most evil looking men they had ever seen.

"Look here me lads," one of them shouted. "It looks as if we have some more Christ killers here."

Sadly, there is no happy ending to this episode. In this way all the adult male Alvaro and Mendoza men were slaughtered and to add horror to horror when the three women went out to search for their men folk later that day, they met with what was possibly an even more horrific end.

Chapter thirty one

A Visitor to the Reeks

Ireland 1996

Dalia and Joseph had decided not to alert the family in McGillicuddys Reeks to their intended visit. As part of her Embassy duties she had visited parts of Southern Ireland before but these trips were limited to the main towns such as Cork and Waterford. She knew the beauty of the countryside, so green and so different from Israel. Of course in Israel there were vast expanses of greenery but these had been created by the early Zionist pioneers with their determination to see forests and vegetation grow in abundance in what had been desert. Here in Ireland all the greenery was the natural result of a heavy rainfall and a temperate climate.

The Reeks came as a bit of a shock. Suddenly from lush rolling hills of meadow and farm land she was confronted with black ominous looking hills as starved of vegetation as her own beloved Negev back home. Slowly Joseph eased the rented Escort up and down the hilly, narrow, badly maintained roads. Eventually the terrain began to flatten out a little and she saw they were approaching a village. All the buildings were constructed in local stone and this included the pub, general store and tiny church. Most of the houses were single storey terraces but there were just three larger detached homes on the edge of town.

"This is the village of Ballymagee and that is the home of my distant cousin Jack Allbarrow," Joseph explained pointing to one of the detached houses.

Dalia had wondered what Joseph's family would be like. Mary, his mother, was a sweet kind and sensitive woman and although her speech displayed a lack of education, Dalia liked her immensely. Dalia judged people for themselves not for their possessions or background. . Now she was seeing the house of a cousin that indicated a comfortable modern lifestyle, albeit miles away from any city. She was not usually impressed by wealth but she was used to a reasonable standard of living. Joseph always painted such a bleak picture of his own home and she hoped that his family home would be something like that of cousin Jack even if a little more modest.

Joseph drove through the village without stopping and they made their way for what seemed like an eternity along a narrow rocky trail, just wide enough for one small car. Dalia could see the black hills again and after an hour of slow progress Joseph stopped the car in what appeared to be the middle of nowhere.

"I'm afraid we must walk from here," he explained.

They climbed out of the car and Joseph made to carry both their overnight bags.

"I'll take my own," Dalia smiled pulling her holdall from his grasp. "After all it is only two weeks since you were lying in a hospital bed."

"I'm fine," Joseph replied, smiling but he already knew Dalia's determination and they made off down the rough footpath together each carrying his own bag.

When eventually the stone house came in to view, it appeared at first to be even worse than Dalia had been led to expect. However, they had travelled a very long way to see Joseph's family and Dalia was not about to be put off by a house that seemed to be totally dilapidated and hundreds of years old. The front door was made out of heavy sturdy oak with huge black hinges and a latch that gave access from without the property. *No lock or other kind of security,* Dalia realised in amazement. Nevertheless Joseph knocked on the heavy door rather than clicking open the latch and walking in.

It was early afternoon and being summertime, the sun was high in the sky. They seemed to have waited for an eternity before there was a response. Joseph uttered not a word as they stood there but just turned to her and smiled in a way that said, be patient.

Eventually the huge door swung open and a man of about fifty years of age stood there regarding them, first suspiciously and then with incredulity. He was quite tall with dark wavy hair that was turning grey at the temples. His eyes were dark brown. His skin was tanned by the elements to an almost leathery hue.

"Joseph," the man eventually gasped. "What in the name of all the saints are you doing here?"

The man made no attempt to invite them into the house and just stood speechless surveying the pair as if he had never before seen their species.

Joseph broke the silence.

"May we come in?"

"Yes, yes, of course," the man replied and mumbled "such a surprise, such a surprise!" as he ushered them into the large dark room that doubled as a hallway, dining room and sitting room.

Dalia wondered who this man might be. At first sight she was sure he must be Joseph's father but there were no hugs or kisses or even a vestige of a smile emanating from his handsome but surly face.

"Sit, sit!" he said pointing to an ancient sofa.

Then Joseph spoke, "So Dad, how are you?"

So this was his father. Dalia was amazed. She wondered where Mary might be and found it almost beyond her imagination to see the two of them as a couple. Physically there was a resemblance to Joseph, she decided, but he was so stern and cold. Joseph may have been shy but even that first day on the bus, he had proved to possess a quiet charm and reserved warmth in his demeanour.

"I'm well enough," the man answered gruffly, "but how are you? Your mother tells me you are mending alright now."

He had ignored Dalia and as Joseph obviously felt so uncomfortable in his father's presence that he had forgotten to introduce her, she decided to take the initiative.

"My name is Dalia Mendoza," she began. "I work at the Israeli Embassy in Dublin."

This information was greeted with a laconic, "I see." No expression of being pleased to meet her; no question as to what she was doing there. Not even any apparent interest in her relationship with his son.

Dalia decided to try a different tack.

"Do you know your son is a hero and nearly died saving the lives of a busload of people?"

This brought a nod as a response and then suddenly the man jumped up and ran through a doorway at the rear of the room. Then to their amazement they heard the sound of sobbing and there was no doubt it was Joseph's father crying like a baby. The hard man was human after all.

Just a minute later the front door of the house opened and in came Mary. Once she had recovered from the shock of seeing them there they embraced and she sat down with them.

"What a wonderful surprise it is to see you both here," she ventured. Then turning to Joseph she asked if he had seen his father.

At that moment the door to the rear opened and in came Aron. He had obviously washed away the tears from his face but he still looked stern. Dalia thought she could just discern a slight softening of the expression in his eyes.

"Hello Mary," he said. "The good Lord has brought him back to us."

"Yes," she replied "and have you met Dalia? I told you about her when I came home from Israel."

Aron nodded curtly and said, "As a friend of my son who has been kind to him I thank you."

Turning to face Joseph he continued,

"Now Miss Mendoza has brought you home, I trust you will be staying for good. Get settled in your old room and give the lady a cup of tea before she leaves."

Before Joseph could answer Aron turned to his wife and said,

"Send one of the children over to the Meadows house to fetch their daughter Mary. We can arrange for our Joseph to marry her once they have been introduced to each other again."

"You remember her don't you Joseph?" he enquired.

Joseph surveyed his father with a look approaching horror.

"Dad, to be sure you know that I have made my career in the Irish Army. You must also know that I cannot possibly spend the rest of my life here. At the moment I am based in Israel and I have grown to love the country and its people. When my time with the army is over I will probably stay in Israel."

The expression on Aron's face was one of utter disgust.

"So you would rather live with the Jews than with your own family and people, would you?"

Dalia was witnessing the beginning of what looked like a very unpleasant full-scale family argument.

"I will go and have a walk outside while you talk," she said as she rose to make for the door.

"No, please stay here," Joseph responded.

"No, she is right," Mary interrupted, trying to make light of the developing situation but not really succeeding. "Come on Dalia, we women will leave this discussion in the hands of the men."

Chapter Thirty Two

Baptism

The Reeks 1610

Aharon at fourteen years old found himself the head of two families comprising a total of nine children all under ten years old.

He knew, when no one returned, that something terrible had happened to his parents and to all the adult members of both families. But he knew that his first responsibility was to the children. For five days he remained terrified in the cave until he heard voices near the entrance to their hiding place. With the assistance of Sarah Meendow, a thankfully mature and sensible nine year old, they ushered all the rest of the children to the very back of the cave and told them to hide quietly behind the piles of provisions. The voices grew louder until Aharon realised they were the recognisable voices of some of the villagers. Aharon peered out from his hiding place and could clearly see four familiar faces from Ballymagee. He stood up and ran crying with relief to the nearest villager who turned out to be Father O'Connor from the little church.

"Terrible, terrible things have happened in these parts these last few days. Rory O'Hara and his men murdered six of our good Catholic men for no good reason. And, my poor boy, I must tell you they murdered all your family. You poor children are alone in the world."

Father O'Connor, unlike some of his predecessors was fond of the Jewish families. He knew they rejected Jesus but they did pray to God. *To be sure,* he often reminded himself, *was not the saviour himself born a Jew?*

It was over a hundred years since the Jews had arrived and he had heard tell how they had brought with them a number of God-fearing Christians whose descendants now helped to swell his little congregation? He also knew from the survivors of that terrible day, only a week earlier, how Joseph had saved the lives of a number of his parishioners. The Father was resolved to help the Jewish children to rebuild their shattered lives.

All the villagers in Ballymagee were also determined to help. The villagers had wanted the children to come and live in Ballymagee but Aharon with rare strength of character in one so young had prevailed. For the next ten years all of the children lived together in the Alvaro house. There were frequent visitors from the village, including Father O'Connor who, although he liked the Jews as people, still felt himself duty bound to convert them to Christianity. However, he never openly broached the subject and just waited for his moment to arrive.

Aharon, in the meantime, learned well the arts of husbandry and shepherding. By the time he was twenty years old he had one of the finest flocks of sheep in the area.

In 1610 Sarah Meendow discussed with Aharon the possibility of her family returning to their own stone house. Not surprisingly Aharon and Sarah had become very close and it was decided that once the oldest Meendow son Joshua was old enough to look after the family Sarah would become the bride of Aharon.

It was Sarah and Aharon who laid down the rules that would govern the matrimonial arrangements of the families for the next three hundred and fifty years. It was also Aharon and Sarah who eventually agreed to the baptism of all the members of the families by a now aged Father O'Connor.

Aharon and Sarah were old enough to know that they were Jews but they could remember very little of the traditions. Aharon desperately wanted to maintain his religious inheritance but needed far more out of religion than just a Saturday morning bible reading. Moreover there would be no other men for many years able to share any kind of religious ceremony.

Aharon never told Sarah what had happened to the scroll of the Torah. This information he took with him to the grave. However both families knew better than to tamper with the flagstones at the end of the garden, whatever they concealed.

Once the baptisms had been completed the families set out to be model Christians.

However, Aharon was determined that the only two Jewish customs he remembered, Friday night candles and some words whose meaning he did not understand but seemed to be some kind of Grace after Meals would remain in the families. Sarah and her younger brother Chaim were delighted to hold on to something of their old lives, from when their parents were alive. The lighting by the oldest girl or eventually by the mother of two candles on a Friday night was instituted as a private tradition. However, it was only to take place in the two stone houses.

As for the Grace, Aharon remembered his father Joseph always solemnly intoning *Nvarech She'achalnu Mishelo* at the end of their Sabbath meals. Again this tradition was continued in both the stone houses from generation to generation but never in other family dwellings. Eventually it was shortened or corrupted into *NBAREK.*

Aharon and Sarah lived good productive lives and died within three months of each other in the year 1664. They were the first members of the families to be buried in the tiny churchyard in Ballymagee. By this time there were a number of children and grandchildren of the two families to bid farewell to their patriarch and matriarch.

So came into being two Christian families eventually known as the Allbarrows and the Meadows. They were both religious Catholic families but with some strange, quaint private customs and an earth shattering secret that lay hidden, undisturbed for hundreds of years, in the ground at the back of the Alvaro house. The only way that succeeding generations would know that there was any significance in the central marked flagstone was because Aharon impressed upon his oldest son in particular and all of his children to a lesser extent, the holiness of the site.

"You only go there to pray in time of great problems, he repeated over and over again to his first born son, another Joseph. You must tell this to your son and grandson and make sure Meadows sons also know this."

"If you do have cause to go there, you will pray directly to the Almighty, not through Jesus."

Pious Catholic sons of the two families were always somewhat shocked to receive this instruction but it was, nevertheless carried out to the letter.

Chapter Thirty Three

A Walk in the Garden.

The Reeks 1996

The word 'garden' was really a misnomer. The area was rough and rock strewn. There were substantial areas under cultivation and these were planted with a mixture of basic vegetables, such as potatoes, carrots and lettuce. It was more like a small farm, Dalia decided. Between the long cultivated beds there was a path of a kind. If anything it was even rougher than the route they had taken from the car but just about navigable with great care.

"We may as well walk down this way," Mary said. "I will show you all the different crops I grow here."

"Are you responsible for all this?" Dalia asked in amazement.

"To be sure," Mary answered. "It is the woman's job to grow the vegetables and the men folk look after the sheep. We have lived like this in both our family and our kinsmen the Meadows family for more years than we know."

"I must explain," she continued, "Joseph is the first born and like his father and grandfather before him he was expected to marry a Meadows girl and become head of the family."

"Joseph really broke my husband's heart by running off to join the army, you know."

"I think I must also tell you that Aron is not very keen on your people. The priest we have here now has told him over and over again that we now understand that Jesus was crucified by the pagan Romans not by the Jews. In fact Father Murphy was after telling me when I came back from Israel last week that the Holy Father has only good things to say about your people."

"But Aron won't accept that. He thinks he knows better than the priests."

By this time the two women had walked to the very end of the semi-cultivated area. Ahead of them the land began to rise steeply. Then Dalia saw the ancient flagstones.

"What are those?" she enquired, "Gravestones?"

"No," Mary answered, "that is our holy site. Whenever there is serious trouble in the family we come here to pray."

"What is written on the stones?" Dalia enquired peering over towards them.

"To be sure we do not know. It is something very holy and has been there for hundreds of years."

"May I approach to have a look?" Dalia enquired anxious not to offend Mary's religious sensibilities.

Dalia badly needed to cement her friendship with Mary. Now that she had met Aron she could see exactly what Joseph was up against. He was obviously a fanatic. She had met too many people in her own country, both Arabs and Jews, who were blinded by what they saw to be their religious obligations. People like Aron were quite certain that only they possessed the true path to the Almighty.

"No stranger has ever been up here before," Mary explained, "but I cannot see what harm there is in taking a look, as long as you don't try to pray there. That is only for our families and only in time of deep trouble."

The centuries of wind and rain had wreaked havoc with the inscriptions. As a result Dalia was unable to decipher anything of it at first. The central stone of the five was the only one where there appeared to be the remains of discernible lettering.

Strange, she thought, *the letters look more like Hebrew than Latin script. Maybe it is some old form of Gaelic writing.* Then with a shock that made her shiver she realised that one word was leaping out of the worn engraving and that word was TORAH.

She must have turned a deathly, ashen white, as she stood transfixed by the discovery.

She dimly heard Mary saying, "Dalia, what is wrong. You look ill. Maybe I should not have let you go up to the holy stone. I hope God is not angry with us."

"No, no," Dalia muttered, "I must take a closer look."

She squatted down and there was absolutely no doubt about it. The words TORAH and MOSHE were visible and by feverishly rubbing the dirt off the stone she quickly uncovered the word YISRAEL.

She turned to her companion and asked, "Can we get a brush and some soapy water from the house?"

Mary quickly realised what Dalia had in mind.

"No Dalia, we cannot mess with the holy stone. It has lain like this for hundreds of years. Can you read anything on it anyway?"

"Yes, yes, yes," Dalia answered, almost shrieking with excitement.

"It is written in my language, Hebrew, the ancient language of the bible. I can already make out three words."

"How can that be? Are you sure? What are they?" Mary demanded in wonderment.

"*TORAH* which means both the law and the first five books of what you call the Old Testament," Dalia explained.

"*MOSHE,* the Hebrew name for Moses and *YISRAEL*-Israel."

"Are you sure?" Mary repeated. "Maybe they just look like Hebrew words."

"If you don't believe me let us bring Joseph out here. He does not read Hebrew but he will certainly recognise the word for Israel. He sees it every day of his life in my country."

"Aron will never permit this," Mary replied, her face clouding over with anxiety.

"Come on," Dalia said. "I will persuade Joseph quietly providing I can get him out of earshot of Aron."

When the two women entered the stone house they found the two men, father and son, sitting in stony silence, glaring at each other.

"Joseph," Dalia ventured, with an anxious glance towards the scowling Aron. "Can I speak to you outside?"

Joseph was more than relieved to have an excuse to leave his father's presence. He stood up and briskly followed Dalia out of the house.

Mary had always held her husband in awe but the trip to Israel and her friendship with Dalia had given her new confidence. She now knew there was a lot more to life than growing vegetables and breeding children in the Reeks. She took one glance at Aron and followed her son and Dalia back outside.

Dalia was determined not to drop even one solitary hint as to why she wanted the three of them to walk up to the end of the garden. She was excited and intrigued by the discovery. She knew far better than Joseph what was chiselled into the stone but for Mary's sake she wanted his corroboration.

Joseph was drained and upset by his altercation with his father. When he had left the Reeks the first time, his father was sad but looked upon his absence as the will of God. He was convinced that Joseph would, with the Almighty's help, get this nonsense out of his system and return to take his rightful place as the Allbarrow's first born.

Mary was also sad. She had spent most of her adult life deferring to her husband. But she loved her son and now, after her recent trip, understood far better why Joseph wished to travel. The three of them remained wrapped up in their own thoughts until Joseph suddenly realised where they were.

"Mother," he said, "why have you brought Dalia to the holy stones? You know only the family can pray here."

Before Mary could answer Dalia spoke up.

"Joseph, will you please take a look at the centre stone and tell me if you can read anything there."

Joseph as a child had often tried to decipher the writing but obviously without success.

"Dalia," he said, "no one can read it. It is very worn and written in some strange script."

"Joseph," Dalia replied, "just bend down and take a look."

"No," Joseph said after complying with the request, "it just looks like it always did."

Dalia bent down besides him and pointed to the word YISRAEL.

"Don't you recognise that word?" she asked.

Joseph peered at the word and suddenly he recognised it. Where he had lived for the previous three years every government document, every banknote, every public notice contained this word.

"Oh my goodness," he exclaimed in astonishment, "That is the Hebrew word for Israel."

"How can our holy stone be engraved with Hebrew?" he gasped.

"Dalia, what do the other words say?"

"I can only make out *TORAH* and *MOSHE* but if I clean it up I may be able to make out the rest," she explained.

Joseph suddenly bethought himself, "We must tell my father."

Aron, not surprisingly regarded the idea of the script being Hebrew as nonsense. It was probably a trick to somehow get him to accept that Joseph would return to

Israel. That was until they almost frogmarched him back to the stone and showed him the word alongside Dalia's passport.

"This is some kind of a sign," Aron decreed sternly when he finally accepted the evidence of his own eyes. "We must pray here for the Lord's guidance."

As on the previous occasion, three years ago, when Joseph had wanted to join the army, the two men stood motionless in front of the stones. This time however, the two women stood equally motionless behind them and they all waited for guidance from above.

After an eternity of silence Aron spoke.

"This middle stone is here for a reason. What that is, God will reveal. There is something buried beneath it and I feel we are now meant to find out what that is."

CHAPTER THIRTY FOUR

REVELATION AND REALISATION.

THE REEKS 1996

Dalia had never been as excited about any event in her entire life.

Joseph was overcome with curiosity.

Mary approached the dig with a mixture of misapprehension and anticipation.

From the minute **Aron** had pronounced that the stone must be lifted he had metamorphosed into an entirely different being. He too was more than a little fearful of the outcome. What if he had made a terrible mistake and by disturbing a holy place he would burn in hell? Strangely, despite this fear he felt strangely relieved as if a great weight was being lifted from his shoulders. He had always made his own decisions and acted upon them. True to lift the stone was his decision but the action this time would be shared with three others.

Lifting the slab proved to be much more difficult than they had thought. It was considerably thicker than the surface above ground had indicated. As a result it was extremely heavy and once the earth had been dug away from round it, it took the combined strength of the two men to lever it upwards.

The result was initially disappointing. All there appeared to be under the slab was a vast quantity of rubble. However, it would hardly be logical to chisel out words on a stone to cover up rubble and they started to dig out the collection of small rocks and stones. Then Joseph's shovel hit something solid and they re-doubled their efforts to remove all the loose material. Finally they cleared the top of an oak chest with heavy metal bands for added security. It was of the type favoured by mariners in earlier times. The chest was still surrounded by impacted earth and it took the two men the best part of a further hour to loosen it sufficiently to lift it from its long-time resting place. At last the task was complete and it needed the combined strength of the four of them to drag the heavy chest out of the pit.

The next task was to open it. There was no lock but the lid was well and truly wedged to make a secure weather-tight closure. Aron was forced to return to the house for tools appropriate to the job. Eventually, with a considerable amount of effort, the lid was prised off. The trio of Allbarrows, together with Dalia, were astonished to see a heavy drum shaped object covered in tarpaulin lying inside the chest. As Joseph lifted the object the cover fell away exposing the most beautiful ornate gold filigree object.

"A Tik Sepher Torah," Dalia gasped. "How beautiful! But I have never seen one as wonderful as this. And how long can this have been hidden from view?"

Joseph had seen this type of scroll before in Israel. His friend Rabbi Yossi had pointed out the variation in outer appearance between the various types of scrolls of the Torah. This scroll was of the kind favoured by Sephardim, Jews who originated in the Middle East or Iberia. Lovingly he lifted it out of the chest and it was then that Mary noticed a thick leather bound book had been lying beneath it. She lifted it out and was amazed to discover it was an ancient Hebrew bible.

She tried to open it and realised that many of the pages were yellow and splitting as she turned them over. However, the last few pages did not contain printed text but rather some kind of hand written account and these pages seemed to be in the best condition.

Joseph carried the scroll back to the house and Mary brought back the bible. The two items were then laid on the old oak dining table, which had seen hundreds of years of family meals. What none of them could possibly have known was that both the scroll and the bible had rested on this self same table many times in the dim and distant past.

The hand-written pages at the back of the bible were written in two different alphabets. The initial entries were all written in Hebrew and Dalia read them out loud to the three Allbarrows. The very first names were Yosef (Jose) ben Shimon Alvaro and his wife Rivka (Rebecca) bat Shlomo followed by the names of their children. The grandchildren's names were inscribed in the Latin text always used for Spanish and other west European languages. The family tree, as such it was, continued until the year 1600 when it came to an abrupt end.

Leafing forward a few pages Joseph found long accounts written in a language that appeared to be Spanish which none of them could understand. What they described would have to wait until a translator could be found.

Aron, after listening to all this in astonished silence suddenly and quite uncharacteristically shouted out,

"'Alvaro,' did you say Alvaro?"

Dalia checked the Hebrew script again and confirmed that was the name.

"Alvaro-Allbarrow," Aron exclaimed. "It is the same name. What was the other name you read out from the Hebrew?"

"Mendoza," Dalia repeated.

"Mendoza-Meadows," Aron shouted out now even more excited. "In the name of sweet Jesus do you realise we must all be Jews."

Although Dalia was as overwhelmed by the discoveries as any of them, she could not suppress a giggle at the use of the

Christian saviour's name in this context. Nor could she resist pointing out to the badly shaken Aron that if they really were Jews, they would have to stop invoking the name Jesus in their conversation.

All these events had occurred on a Thursday and by now it had grown dark outside. This was the thick, impenetrable almost tangible darkness where there is no light outside for miles. Dalia was suddenly aware of the darkness and the silence that seemed to descend with the night. She realised that there had been very few occasions in her entire lifetime when she had been unable to pick up a single sound emanating from outside.

The new and ever more independent Mary without a glance in the direction of her husband interjected,

"Dalia I don't know what your intentions were but everything seems changed now. How long were you planning on being away from the embassy in Dublin?"

"Joseph was going to stay on with you for a few days and I was hoping I could stay with you till tomorrow morning and then return to Dublin," Dalia explained.

"You can stay as long as you want," came an invitation from a most unlikely source, namely Aron.

"Thank you Aron," replied the somewhat surprised Dalia. "Maybe," she continued after a moment, "I could stay till Sunday."

"Of course," answered the now transformed Aron.

The Torah scroll and the bible were gently placed in a cupboard and the four waited for the return of the other Allbarrow children.

It was decided that Dalia would sleep with the oldest Allbarrow daughter. She was called Bridget and returned from a visit to the Meadows house further along the coast, with the three youngest members of the family later that evening. The children were thrilled to find their big brother Joseph at home and wanted to fire all manner of questions at him. These he parried and told them that there would be lots to tell them later on.

Alan, Joseph's brother also returned late after a hard day trying to find better pasture for the family sheep.

When all five of their younger children were finally present Aron called a family meeting. Firstly he had to introduce Dalia to Alan and Bridget and the others. That was the easy part. Then Aron set about, in his own way, to tell of the momentous events that had occurred that day. His two children heard him out in silence. They had never before seen their father so happy or so animated.

Then at the end Alan asked,

"Does that make us Jews then?"

Dalia interrupted before Aron could answer,

"You must realise that all this will need to checked by Rabbis before you are accepted. What you probably don't understand is that being Jewish is dependent on the mother not the father. If there is one non-Jewish mother in the chain that will break the link."

Aron spoke again. "It is up to the Almighty. It was a miracle that we decided to dig up the chest and we must all follow his will."

CHAPTER THIRTY FIVE

JOURNEY'S END

ISRAEL 1997

The marriage of Joseph and Dalia took place in Jerusalem in June1997. Joseph's friend and now distant kinsman, Rabbi Yossi Alvaro, performed the outdoor ceremony. The sun shone down from a cloudless blue sky and Joseph felt as if his whole life and that of his entire family for over five hundred years had all been leading him back to the ancient homeland from which his ancestors had set sail almost two thousand years previously.

As Rabbi Yossi chanted the traditional blessings for the Bride and Groom, Joseph felt that no human being could ever deserve as much happiness as he experienced that day.

The newspapers in Israel, Ireland and Spain had been full of their story.

Some had made the amazing family epic the centrepiece of their articles where others had been keen to emphasise the romantic tale of the discovery of the Sepher Torah.

The ancient scroll had been taken to Israel where a scribe had carefully and lovingly checked it. He had pronounced it to be in perfect condition and it was agreed that it should occupy pride of place in the Ark of a beautiful new Sephardic synagogue where Rabbi Yossi had recently been appointed resident Rabbi. If old Rabbi Yair ben Moshe, who had lost his life to protect the holy scroll, five hundred years ago, could look down from heaven, his joy would have been beyond measure.

And what of all the previous generations of Allbarrows and Meadows whose blood ran in Joseph's veins? They too would know that all their suffering had not been in vain.

By this time a good percentage of the villagers of Ballymagee had ancestors from the two families. This was mixed with good Irish and Spanish Christian stock. These people could not be considered to be Jews nor would they have wished to give up their strong Catholic heritage.

However, to establish the maternal blood line of the main members of the two families had needed considerable assistance from the current priest who cared for his flock in the little ancient stone church of Ballymagee. He was Father Patrick Meadows; also a distant relative and he had been born and bred in the village. He had been trained in seminaries in Rome. He had also been the parish priest at a large church in Dublin. There he had met and formed a close friendship with the then Irish Chief Rabbi. Eventually the call of home had decided him to literally beg to be allowed to return to his home village. His superiors in Dublin had been loath to agree but his persistence and longing to return to his roots, had won them over.

The old Hebrew bible of Jose proved that the Jewish families only married among themselves until 1603 when all records ceased. Joseph had then consulted his friend Rabbi Yossi Alvaro who had agreed to help him in his quest to confirm his Jewish identity. He flew over to Ireland and met with Father Meadows. The latter was able to explain that the parish priests had always kept parish records even as far back as the late sixteenth century of births, marriages and deaths in the tiny isolated community of Ballymagee. In addition many of the inscriptions on the ancient gravestones were still legible. It had thus been possible to construct family trees for both the Allbarrows and the Meadows. These proved beyond doubt that the maternal line of Joseph's family originated only from the original Mendoza and Alvaro families.

His friend Rabbi Yossi had arranged for Joseph to be interviewed by senior rabbinical authorities in Israel. There they had presented their evidence. Despite the respect in which Rabbi Yossi was held, the claim, not surprisingly, was very difficult for the Dayanim (religious judges) to accept. However the unbroken chain back to Don Jose Alvaro and Yitzchak Mendoza was indisputable and Joseph won his right to return to the ancient faith of his forefathers. And now he was to marry Dalia, the girl he had met on the Jerusalem bus. Between them they would set up an orthodox Jewish home in Israel.

Aron and Mary attended the wedding but after much discussion they had decided to remain in the Catholic religion of their childhood back in McGillicuddys Reeks. There, their second son Alan was proving himself to be a very successful shepherd. By the turn of the Millennium, Alan was employing two other young men from the village and was exporting his special breed of sheep to England and France.

Aron died of a heart attack in 2003 and the new heir to the Allbarrows was of course Alan. The funeral took place in the little stone church at Ballymagee. Alan had married Mary Meadows and by the time of Aron's death had produced three children. And in both the old stone houses, the traditions still continued for the mother to light two candles on a Friday night, and for the family to recite *NBARECH* after Sunday lunch.

However, the third tradition of visiting the stone slab at the end of the garden, in time of trouble, was no longer possible as the Sepher Torah (scroll of the law) had now returned home to Jerusalem after countless centuries of exile.

Joseph had left the Irish army before his marriage to Dalia. Captain O'Hagan, his commanding officer, had attended the wedding and joined enthusiastically with the other men in dances to honour the bride and groom.

Joseph, however, was still a country boy at heart and he and Dalia settled in a small farm up in the hills outside Jerusalem. There is a nearby village, within easy walking distance, called Beth Nissim. The village contains an ancient synagogue that Joseph attends daily. At the time of writing they have two sons, Shimon and Elazar. Despite her duties as a mother to the two little boys Dalia still travels daily to her job in the Foreign Ministry in Jerusalem. And Joseph is a part time soldier in the Israeli army and a sheep farmer.........

End.